"I'm so sorry—for hurting you, for causing you pain."

"Is that why you sent the flowers?" Beau saw the immediate hurt in her eyes.

"No, it's just another long-overdue apology to someone who deserved better. As for the flowers, I wanted to make you smile."

"The flowers are beautiful," Emery told him. "And thank you for…everything."

"I'm glad I was ▮▮▮

She hesitated. ▮▮▮

"So, did the flo▮▮▮

Her lips tugged ▮▮▮ ▮▮▮ainst her will. "Yes, they did the trick."

The admission pleased him.

It had become important to him in a way that he probably shouldn't spend too much time trying to understand. If he could, he would make her smile every day. Or every hour, if she'd let him.

Not to make amends, but because her smile opened up something inside him.

She felt like the missing piece to his life. The thought shook him, because he hadn't realized until her that anything had been missing.

Brenda Minton lives in the Ozarks with her husband, children, cats, dogs and strays. She is a pastor's wife, Sunday-school teacher, coffee addict and is sleep-deprived. Not in that order. Her dream to be an author for Harlequin started somewhere in the pages of a romance novel about a young American woman stranded in a Spanish castle. Her dreams came true, and twenty-plus books later, she is an author hoping to inspire young girls to dream.

Books by Brenda Minton

Love Inspired

Mercy Ranch

Bluebonnet Springs

Visit the Author Profile page at LoveInspired.com for more titles.

Earning Her Trust

Brenda Minton

LOVE INSPIRED
INSPIRATIONAL ROMANCE

LOVE INSPIRED®
INSPIRATIONAL ROMANCE

ISBN-13: 978-1-335-56768-0

Earning Her Trust

Recycling programs
for this product may
not exist in your area.

For questions and comments about the quality of this book, please contact us
at CustomerService@Harlequin.com.

Love Inspired
22 Adelaide St. West, 41st Floor
Toronto, Ontario M5H 4E3, Canada
www.LoveInspired.com

Printed in U.S.A.

I will praise thee; for I am fearfully and wonderfully made: marvellous are thy works; and that my soul knoweth right well.
—*Psalm* 139:14

Thank you to my editor and my agent, the two Melissas. It's been a fantastic, wonderful journey and I am thankful to the two of you, for guiding me, listening to me and helping me out along the way. I look forward to more adventures!

Chapter One

The brick building that housed the county Division of Family Services always brought back a myriad of emotions for Emery Guthrie. As she stood on the sidewalk on a too-warm day in May, the memories came back stronger than ever. At almost thirty years old, she should no longer be held captive by the past. It had been fifteen years. She'd had many years of good memories to replace the awful ones of her father.

Standing there, leaning on the crutch that she'd been using for all those fifteen years since her escape from her father, Turk Green, his basement, his abuse and his friends, she became the child again. The beaten, broken girl thrown into a basement and left to suffer for weeks.

Absently, she reached to pet her service dog,

Zeb. The chocolate-brown labradoodle understood that touch and he moved close to her side. He grounded her to reality, to the present. She'd been rescued.

Rescued. She drew on that word. She'd been rescued. By this place, this building and the people inside who were often disliked, but sometimes loved. People who had, in her case, done a remarkable job in rescuing her. They'd seen her father jailed for the abuse that had left her physically and emotionally broken. They'd placed her with a foster mother, Nan Guthrie, the woman who had adopted her as a teen, giving her a new last name and a new life. Emery Green had become Emery Guthrie, a girl with hope and a future.

Rescued was also the word that described her faith. Because with God she'd found a new life that, in spite of the brokenness of the past, made her feel whole.

But today wasn't about Emery. It was about the two young girls whom Nan had been caring for the past few weeks. They'd lost their parents in a terrible, violent tragedy. They'd been uprooted from their home, their lives and all they'd ever known, brought to Pleasant, Missouri, and placed with Nan until their new guardian could be found.

That man was Beau Wilde. A grade ahead

of Emery, Beau had spent their school years making her life even more miserable with his bullying.

He'd taunted, teased and humiliated her.

She shook her head, as if freeing herself from the thoughts she'd not allowed to see the light of day in many years. Those memories belonged in the past, which was where she'd kept them until she'd learned that Cadence and Charlie would be living with him.

Just then, a truck pulled off the road and circled the parking lot.

Emery hesitated a moment too long. Beau was out of his truck and heading in her direction. He nodded as he closed in on her.

There wasn't a hint of recognition in his dark eyes as he hurried forward and reached for the door.

"Please, let me." He opened the door and stepped back to allow her to go first. "Nice dog."

"Thank you," she whispered. She cleared her throat. "His name is Zeb."

And my name is Emery, Emery Guthrie. Not Litter Box, not Peg Leg, not Invisible Girl.

He looked at her, as if trying to place her. She would recognize him anywhere. He still wore his dark hair short and crisp. He still had that wide smile that flashed perfect teeth. Even though he wore the pallor of someone who'd been sick, it didn't detract from his looks. He was tall, strong and confident.

He followed her inside the building, and when she glanced back, for a brief moment he didn't look confident. He looked ragged, torn and hurt.

Her heart gave in. "They're in here," she told him, pointing to the family waiting room.

"I'm sorry?"

"Nan and the girls are this way."

"You're the caseworker?"

"No," she said, drawing in a breath. "I'm Emery."

He shook his head, looking confused. He was not the author of her fate. She was not invisible. She wanted to tell him that he'd wounded her but he hadn't kept her from succeeding. She'd gone to college. She'd worked as a state caseworker in a nearby county, and now she was back home with Nan, finding joy in her job as an elementary school counselor.

But her story didn't matter to Beau Wilde.

She pushed the door open and led him inside where Nan waited with Cadence, age six, and Charlie, age fourteen. Emery paused just inside the room and wished, prayed, hoped that something good would come of this day and that God would do for these two girls what He'd done for her: restore their hope, their smiles and their joy.

Nan looked up from the knitting she'd brought

to keep her hands and mind busy. Emery knew Nan had been busy praying, the way she'd always prayed for her foster children. These two girls were probably the last girls Nan would ever foster. Nan's age and her health meant the end of her role as foster parent. She'd taken Charlie and Cadence because it had been temporary and because she'd made a promise to do so, should something happen to their parents.

Garret and Dana had grown up in Pleasant. For Nan, that meant they were family. The last thing their girls needed was to be sent to complete strangers. Or worse, split up and put in separate foster homes.

Emery had worried that it would be too much for the woman who had helped her through a few difficult years as a teenager, a woman they'd all seen as invincible. A woman they now realized was just as human as the rest of them. Nan had dementia. It was early on in her diagnosis and she mostly seemed to be just fine, but there were moments when it became more apparent. There were moments when she became "overset." That was Nan's word for distraught or confused. Nan was fighting hard against the dementia, but in the end, they all knew that the dementia would win.

Charlie gave them a sharp look as she and Beau walked into the room together.

It was safe to say that Charlie was angry. Very angry. She had chopped her hair off with Nan's kitchen scissors and dyed it black with dye she'd picked up at the discount store. She'd also managed to redesign almost all of her clothing, which was why today she wore gray sweatpants and a too-large T-shirt.

"So he finally decided to show up," Charlie said with a glare. "My mom tried to tell my dad that he—"

Emery raised a hand to stop her, then sent Charlie's younger sister a meaningful look. The only thing that would stop Charlie's anger was Cadence. Charlie loved her little sister.

Emery didn't disagree with Charlie. What had Garret Parker been thinking when he'd convinced his wife that in case of their death or inability to care for their children, Beau would be a good substitute parent? Like most people, Garret probably never thought this day would come.

But it had.

The worst had happened. Dana and Garret had been murdered in their own home, and Beau Wilde was now legal guardian to Charlie and Cadence.

"Yes, I'm here," Beau spoke, his voice gentle, unlike the voice of her memories. "I'm so sorry. I…"

He pinched the bridge of his nose and drew in a breath. Zeb, always in tune with emotions, whimpered and moved a few inches in his direction. Absently, his hand moved to the dog's head.

"It's about time," Charlie grumbled.

"I know," he answered. His eyes filled with tears as his gaze landed on Cadence. The little girl had drawn her knees to her chin and her arms were wrapped around her legs. "I'm so sorry," he said, the words thick with emotion.

Barely six, Cadence's strawberry blond hair was a tumble of unruly curls, her sad blue eyes gazing up at him. Emery wanted to hold the child close and protect her from any further sadness. And Charlie. Poor, angry Charlie had held her little sister in a closet as home invaders took the lives of their parents.

Beau closed his eyes, briefly, as grief ravaged his expression.

He'd lost his best friend. He'd come home from a mission trip to claim the children of that friend and to face a very different reality than the one he'd expected.

He gathered his emotions, but it was obviously a struggle.

Emery's own emotions were all over the place. She wanted to protect the girls. She wanted to help them all adjust. She felt an unwelcome wave of compassion for Beau, the man she didn't like or want to care about.

"Come here, Cricket." He held his arms out to Cadence.

The child hesitated at the edge of her seat, her feet tapping as if unsure what direction they wanted to go. Would they go in his direction, stay put or run?

Her feet touched the floor, but only briefly. In the end, she sank back into her seat, her eyes closing as a tear zigzagged down her cheek. Beau's arms dropped to his sides. The caseworker stood, her expression wary as she glanced from guardian to children and then to Nan, who had been appointed temporary foster parent as per Garret and Dana's will.

"We're running late, so we should start our meeting," Mrs. Bridges said.

"Yes, of course," Beau said, his gaze still on Cadence. "I'm sorry. There was traffic."

"Whatever," Charlie snarled. "You're never on time."

"That's enough," Nan warned.

Emery clamped down on recriminations that would have echoed and expanded on Charlie's. *Be the adult*, she told herself. She knew how. She was a school counselor. She was trained to calm frazzled nerves, deal with tense situations and guide children to make better choices.

"But I'm here now and I'm so sorry."

He held his arms out, giving it another shot. Cadence stood, obviously torn but wanting to go to him. Her eyes, liquid with tears, darted from Beau to Charlie.

"Don't," Charlie said with a growl. "He doesn't deserve us."

"Charlie," Emery warned. She looked from the teenager to Beau to Cadence. "Let's take a breath and remember that we're all here to support each other."

"You're not here to support us," Charlie said, sounding close to tears. "You're here to dump us on him."

"Nan and I won't abandon you. We will still be here…" Emery took a step toward the girl. But she moved too quickly and her clumsy left leg, unable to keep up, spasmed. Zeb gave a soft woof and moved to her side, while at the same time, Beau put his hand on her arm to steady her.

"Are you okay?" he asked, his voice too gentle, too kind.

The question brought her gaze up to meet his. His dark eyes seemed sincere and his hand on her arm was strong.

"I'm fine," she faltered. She rested her hand on Zeb's head, her fingers slipping through the soft fur, finding comfort and strength in his nearness.

She took a deep breath and found herself again.

"Emery?" Nan's voice called to her.

Emery nodded, a silent answer to the question that hadn't been asked. Nan knew of his bullying, knew of the depression it had spawned. Could Emery handle being in this meeting with him? She could. It would be good for her to face him, forgive him and move on with her life.

"Now that you're here, we should sit down and talk about the best plan for the girls." Mrs. Bridges seemed a little unsure as she glanced around the room.

"Of course, we should," Emery agreed, and her gaze clashed with Beau Wilde's.

The look made her want to find an exit, but she couldn't. She wouldn't.

The best thing she could do for Charlie and Cadence was to make them feel secure about having Beau Wilde as their guardian. Even if she didn't agree with the decision.

Beau Wilde was shaken to the core by the situation he found himself in. Until his brother had caught up with him last week, he'd had no idea that Garret and Dana had been killed.

The caseworker got his attention.

"Mr. Wilde, if you'd like, we can go to the conference room."

"Conference room," he repeated, because he hadn't really been listening.

"If it's our future, we should be able to listen." Charlie's glare included each of them.

Her anger took him by surprise, but given the situation, it shouldn't. She would never again be the little girl he'd always known.

"Not for this meeting, Charlie," the case-worker said firmly.

"Fine." Charlie grabbed a book off the table. "Anything to keep me out of your hair."

Mrs. Bridges paused in front of the teenager, squatting to put herself at eye level. "We need to be able to have a conversation and you don't need to worry. You are fourteen, Charlie. I want you to be able to resume your life as a teenager and not as a parent."

Beau's heart broke all over again.

Nan patted Charlie on the leg. "I'll sit with you. I'm not really needed in there."

"Nan, are you sure?" Mrs. Bridges asked as she hesitated before leaving the room. "You have more experience than the rest of us put together."

Nan laughed. "I think you'll do just fine without me. And I'll be happier sitting here with Charlie and Cadence."

Beau gave them a last look, then he followed Emery and Mrs. Bridges from the room. They walked a short distance down a dark hall. Mrs. Bridges unlocked the door to the conference room and motioned Beau and Emery in ahead of her.

Beau let Emery and her dog go first. She gave him a thunderous look, her stormy gray eyes matching her expression. Something about that look caused him to hesitate.

This woman did not like him and he couldn't imagine why.

His high school self was someone he'd come to dislike. He'd been spoiled, the son of a cattleman who owned several car dealerships in the tristate area. He'd been self-centered. He hadn't been the person his parents raised him to be.

Then, in his third year in college, his life had changed. He'd gone to church with a friend, and the boy who'd grown up going to church finally met God in a life-changing way. He'd continued to help his father with the family business, but his true calling was mission work.

If he had to guess, the woman who took a seat opposite him at the conference table was someone who hadn't liked him in high school and didn't plan on liking him now.

"Where do we start?" he asked while the caseworker shuffled through papers. He'd flown into Kansas City and he'd met with Garret's lawyer. He'd been fully apprised of the situation he was about to walk into.

"Mr. Wilde, the girls have obviously been through a traumatic experience," Mrs. Bridges said.

Did she think he was unaware of that fact? He'd read newspaper articles. He'd read police reports. He knew what Charlie and Cadence had experienced. As he'd read those reports, he'd lived through the experience with them, feeling their fear, their loss, their anger.

The fact that he hadn't been here didn't mean he didn't care. He never expected to come home and find that one of his high school friends, along with his wife, had been murdered. He hadn't expected to raise two children.

"Mr. Wilde?" The caseworker cleared her throat to get his attention.

"I think I understand what the girls have been through." He took a calming breath. "I'm very aware of the nightmare they lived through. I'm devastated by the loss of my friend and his wife."

"The Parkers' wish was for you to raise their daughters," the caseworker continued.

"Yes, I am aware of that also." He looked down at his hands, not really recognizing them as his own. He'd lost a lot of weight while in the hospital in Africa. "But maybe the girls would be better with Nan and Emery."

"Yes, maybe they would," Emery spoke up, and with those words, he recognized her and he knew why she disliked him.

He couldn't get lost in the past, in the torture he'd inflicted on this woman, but shame washed over him as he stared at her, remembering.

He switched his focus back to the caseworker. Raising two girls would definitely be outside his wheelhouse of expertise. If he raised the girls, they'd have to move to Tulsa. If he raised them, it would be in a single-parent home. Young girls had a whole lot of stuff they'd go through. He felt heat rush to his cheeks just thinking about it.

All of that and the added trauma of losing their parents. That part stopped him, made him think about their pain and not his own concerns. The loss and the heartache that Charlie and Cadence were experiencing was unimaginable and far more important than his discomfort. Did he know how to help them navigate that loss?

He would have to find help for them.

"Mr. Wilde, I'm assuming the Parkers discussed their decision with you, to leave the girls in your care if something should happen to them?" Mrs. Bridges asked him in an impatient tone.

"Yes, they did. None of us ever thought this moment would happen."

"But it did happen. In a way that no one would ever have imagined. The girls are lost, hurting and frightened. They need stability and permanency."

"I understand that." He glanced across the table, seeking something from Emery Guthrie. Maybe he wanted her to step in and say what they all knew—this was a terrible idea.

Instead, she seemed to be at war with herself. In the end, rather than speaking up, she shook her head.

"I have a suggestion that I'd like to propose," Mrs. Bridges told him as she tapped her pen on the table and studied him.

"I'm open to suggestions." He studied the woman in the seat across from him. Emery Guthrie with her straight dark hair framing an expressive face.

Do you roll in the litter box before you come to school? Why do you even bother getting up each day?

The words ricocheted in his mind. She might have been twelve or thirteen at the time he'd said that to her. It had been before her injuries, before Nan. She looked up, meeting his gaze, and a ghost of a smile touched her expression. She hated him.

In that moment, he hated himself.

"The girls will be done with school in two weeks. If they could stay here and finish, that would be best. You would have Nan's help. And Emery's. She's bonded with the girls. She's helped them so much in the few short weeks they've been with Nan."

Emery in his life for the next two weeks, giving him those hurt and angry looks? He deserved it all, but still, it wasn't something to look forward to.

"I have a business to run in Tulsa," he explained as a last-ditch attempt to regain control of the situation. He rubbed his chest, wishing away the pain that settled there. At the moment, he didn't know if it was an aftereffect of the virus that had put him in the hospital, or the guilt of what he'd done to Emery.

"Who's been in charge while you were out of the country all this time?" Emery questioned him.

"The business you need to run?" she prodded when he didn't answer.

The Wilde family owned and managed several dealerships in northeast Oklahoma, Arkansas and southwest Missouri. Each dealership had a general manager. In his Tulsa office, he had a capable assistant. He explained that to them, then he sat back in the chair, breathing in and praying for peace and for wisdom.

He closed his eyes, needing a moment.

"Mr. Wilde?" The caseworker's tone was cautious. He opened his eyes.

"I can stay here in Pleasant until the end of the school year."

"The girls will need to continue their counseling. Charlie is understandably angry. Cadence hasn't spoken in the month since their parents' death," Mrs. Bridges continued, filling him in on details he'd already become aware of. "I would like for them to remain in counseling with Mrs. Graves, the woman they've been seeing. The girls trust her."

"That means driving from Tulsa to Pleasant. How often?" Beau asked.

"Once a week," both the caseworker and Emery responded.

"I see." He was starting to notice a trend, one that appeared to make him the bad guy. "I'll move the girls to my brother's house outside of Pleasant and we'll finish school. And we'll continue to see Mrs. Graves for as long as is necessary."

"I think that's a good plan," Emery said as she pushed to her feet. "Nan will be more than happy to help."

"I'm going to need lots of help," he admitted, also standing. "Girls…"

Emery's expression changed. First compassion and then amusement flickered in her eyes. It caught him by surprise, holding him for a moment, making it difficult to turn away. Before, she'd been stern. The light in her eyes changed her to pretty, possibly captivating.

"Girls can be frightening," she agreed. "And Charlie will keep you on your toes."

He nodded in agreement, but it wasn't Charlie whom he was thinking about. His gaze had strayed to the woman who stood across from him, a woman whom he'd forgotten about until today.

He had two weeks in which to figure out how to raise the girls. That plan included the woman sitting across from him. Emery Guthrie, a woman who clearly disliked him.

They might never be friends, but he'd like the chance to prove that he was no longer the monster of a teen she remembered.

Chapter Two

The drive to the Rocking W Ranch was silent and uncomfortable. Occasionally Beau would glance into the back seat of his truck and make eye contact with Charlie. Cadence kept her attention focused on the window, gazing out at passing farmland, the occasional pond and, once, a deer. He'd heard a startled gasp when she saw the creature. Proof that she could speak. But because of her trauma, she chose not to.

He hadn't been here to attend the funeral. He hadn't been here to comfort the girls. It had been out of his control, the illness that had put him in the hospital, unable to communicate and unable to reach out to family. Because he hadn't been with his group, it had taken the team almost two weeks to locate him.

Once he'd been able to call home, he'd learned that life had taken an unexpected turn during his absence. Unexpected and heartbreaking. He'd flown home as soon as medically possible, landed in Kansas City, where he'd spent a few days learning about what happened to his friends, before driving to Pleasant.

He could hear Charlie whispering to Cadence in the back seat. He couldn't make out all of her words, but he thought she must be reassuring her little sister. Had she whispered to her as they hid in the closet? His heart pounded hard against his chest as he thought of them hiding from the home invaders.

He smiled at the face reflected in the rearview mirror, the face of a young teen trying very hard to appear brave. Her eyes narrowed with a show of false bravado.

"Stop looking at me," she ordered as her arm went around her sister. "Stop thinking you're going to be anything to us."

He remained silent, giving his attention over to the road.

The turn to the Rocking W was ahead. He hit his blinker, then they were on a paved driveway lined by a white vinyl fence. At the end of the lane, he could see the two-story home that his parents had built years ago. The house he'd grown up in. His parents now lived in St. Louis so they could be near his grandmother. They were semiretired and waiting patiently for their sons, now in their early thirties, to give them grandchildren.

His mother, recovering from open-heart surgery, promised him that as soon as she possibly could, she'd be in Pleasant to help with Charlie and Cadence.

"Is this where you live?" Charlie asked, a hint of curiosity hiding in her voice.

"It's where my brother lives."

"Are you homeless?" she asked.

"No, I'm not homeless. My home, as you know, is outside of Tulsa."

"Is it a tent?" she pushed.

"It isn't a tent." He had more than enough room for himself and two girls. He guessed he would also need to find a live-in housekeeper. He had room for one of those, too.

The garage door opened and he pulled in.

"Let's go inside," he said as he climbed out and reached to open the back door. Charlie had already pushed it open. She hopped out and then helped her sister.

He wasn't needed, so he grabbed the suitcases out of the bed of the truck. In the distance, a goat called out a greeting and a half dozen head of cattle answered. Cadence turned to the open garage door, trying to catch a glimpse of the livestock. She likely didn't have much experience with farm life. Their father, Garret, raised by a single mom who had passed away during his second year in college, had left Pleasant after high school. Dana's home life had been pretty messed up and over the years her family had scattered to parts unknown.

"We can see the animals later, if you want," he offered.

Cadence peered up at him. He wanted to pick her up, hold her close, comfort her. Charlie had hold of her hand, though, sending the clear message she wasn't going to give an inch in this battle of wills.

"Okay, let's go inside and get you both settled. Are you hungry?" he asked as he pushed the door open, letting them into the hallway off the family room.

He could smell something cooking. Almost as quickly, he realized that something was burning. And then the fire alarm sounded, the ear-piercing shrillness causing the three of them to take a step back.

Over the alarm, Beau could hear his brother, Ethan, yelling at the stove and whatever he'd been trying to cook.

"Is that our food?" Charlie actually giggled.

"I think it might be," he answered.

"I don't know why we couldn't stay at Nan's," Charlie accused. "With Emery. Emery knows how to cook."

"I'm sure Ethan can cook," he assured her. "This is probably an off day."

"Sure it is," she said.

Curiosity obviously won out over skepticism, because she followed him through the house, Cadence's hand securely in her own. Their steps slowed as they walked through the family room to the kitchen. His parents had remodeled during Ethan's and Beau's teen years. The family room had become the hangout room, with a projector screen for movie nights, a pool table and tons of board games in a closet. Weekends had always seen the house full of teens.

The family room opened into the kitchen and breakfast nook. That was where they found Ethan in a haze of smoke, the now-quiet smoke alarm in his hand and a pan sizzling in the sink.

"Dinner?" Beau asked with a chuckle.

"If you like blackened grilled cheese," Ethan answered. He smiled at the girls. "Hello."

No response. Charlie had backed out of the room to the somewhat fresher air of the family room. Cadence stood next to her.

"You know Charlie and Cadence?" Beau asked.

Ethan nodded. "Nan had me over for dinner last week."

The girls stared without responding.

"I wanted to have dinner ready when you got

here. I know it's early, but I thought they might be hungry."

"We'll figure something out," Beau said as he turned to draw the girls back to the kitchen. "Cereal?"

"You can't feed kids cereal for dinner," Charlie informed him. "We need protein and vegetables."

"Of course."

Suddenly he heard the sound of liquid dripping on tile. Then Cadence as she started to cry.

Charlie gasped and shot Beau an accusing look. "You made her wait too long. Six-year-olds can't wait so long."

"I…" Beau didn't know what he was supposed to say. He caught the towel his brother tossed his way. "Let's get you cleaned up, Cricket."

The nickname caught her attention and she gave him a hesitant nod with just a hint of a smile.

He put the towel on the floor, then he knelt in front of the child. Tears were streaming down her cheeks. Charlie stood behind her, looking belligerent. Or was it triumphant, as if she'd known he would fail?

Cadence sniffled, drawing his attention back to the problem at hand. He gave her a gentle smile and her lips trembled, as if she was trying her best to be strong.

"Don't worry, we've got this, Cadence," he looked to her sister. "Charlie, could you help me find some clean clothes?"

"Sorry, you're going to have to figure this out on your own." Charlie marched off, making herself at home in the family room. She was proving her point the only way a fourteen-year-old knew how. He guessed this was her way of sending the message that he shouldn't be raising two girls.

Cadence continued to cry without making a sound. Her lips were clamped shut as tears raced down her cheeks. She didn't move to wipe them away. A paper towel appeared in his line of sight. Ethan handed it over and Beau used it to wipe the tears away.

"We have to get you changed and then we'll find something to eat." Beau stared at her, not quite sure of the first step in this process. "I bet you need to get cleaned up. How about a bath?"

He heard balls clash as Charlie took a shot at the pool table in the family room. Cadence needed to be cleaned up. Charlie needed discipline. They all needed something to eat.

"You want me to call Nan?" Ethan offered as he settled himself on a bar stool at the island.

"Probably a good idea." Beau remained squatted down in front of Cadence. Her tears had dried and she stared at him with liquid blue eyes full of sorrow and shame. "It's okay, honey. Floors clean up and so do little girls. Listen, you're going to have to help me out because I'm clueless. I can change out the engine in a car, but I'm pretty lost when it comes to kid stuff."

She smiled a little.

"Nan isn't home," Ethan said.

"Great," Beau muttered. "Okay, bath first. Which suitcase is yours?"

She pointed at the bright pink bag with sequins.

"Emery will be here in ten minutes," Ethan continued.

Beau, still squatting in front of Cadence, briefly lost his balance. Cadence giggled. A real giggle. With sound. He would fall over for a woman any day of the week if he could hear that sound again.

He smiled at her. "So, you like that I'm clumsy."

She nodded, barely.

Ethan cleared his throat. "I think it was about you falling over the second I said Emery's name. I almost giggled, too, but I'm thirty-three. That would be weird."

"Why don't you go cook something," Beau shot back.

"No need. Emery said Nan keeps frozen

meals in the freezer. She'll bring one over. I just have to preheat the oven."

"I told you Emery knows how to take care of kids," Charlie called out from the family room.

"Yeah, of course she does," he agreed, even as he shot his brother a warning look. "But I'm pretty sure Emery doesn't want to be involved in this situation."

Ethan shrugged. "She seemed okay. I mean, we all know you're a jerk, so it isn't like we're surprised that she isn't your number one fan."

"I'm not a jerk."

Ethan's mirth dissolved to seriousness. "But high school was another matter."

Beau rose to his full six feet and held a hand out to Cadence. She slipped her small fingers into his hand and something shifted. Maybe every now and then things would be okay.

Cadence reached for her suitcase. Beau took it from her and together they walked down the hall to the nearest bathroom, where he ran the water, making sure it wasn't too hot, and then he would leave Cadence to get cleaned up.

Emery would arrive and she would probably gloat, because, like Charlie, she had known that he would fail at this parenting thing. The idea of her finding pleasure in his failure only reinforced his desire to succeed. He would not fail at this. And he wouldn't fail at finding a way to change Emery's opinion of him.

For some reason, it had suddenly become very important to him that she not see him for the person he used to be.

The last place Emery wanted to be was the Rocking W Ranch. Yet here she stood, on the front porch of the Wildes' beautiful, large home. She remembered as a kid on the school bus wondering what it would feel like to walk through the doors of this house every afternoon after school. What would it be like to come home to a mom who smelled of perfume and not smoke and booze? A mom who stayed and didn't leave one summer, never to return? Or coming home to a dad who didn't hit? A dad who didn't think a baseball bat served as a good disciplinary object? A dad who didn't laugh when his friends…

She shook off those thoughts and the cold chill that accompanied the memories.

Some people had "summer vacation" kind of lives. That was what she'd always called these functional, decent families. They were the families who posted fun pictures on social media. Beach pictures. Lake pictures. Grand Canyon pictures. Family pictures with parents and kids laughing as if life was perfect.

Children like Emery had nothing but fear for their childhood memories. Fear and insecurity.

As a school counselor, she tried to educate adults who hadn't lived her existence, helping them to understand children whose lives were far removed from anything they'd ever experienced. The children from dysfunctional homes weren't responsible for their dirty hair, their smelly clothes or the moments when they couldn't stay awake for math. They were hungry, tired and frightened. They were surviving the best way they knew how without the aid of parents who should be helping them with those basic needs.

Stop, she told herself. She needed to focus on going inside this house. She leaned on her crutch, Zeb at her side. He moved closer, whimpering a little as he absorbed her mood and tried to bring comfort. She rested her right hand on the top of his head and he gave her an imploring look.

"Okay, God." She looked up. "We've got this. I am fearfully and wonderfully made. And You're right, so is he." Ugh, what a thing to have to admit.

She rang the doorbell.

A moment later the door opened. Ethan Wilde smiled down at her from his overwhelming height. She liked Ethan. After having grown up in a bigger church somewhere near Springfield, he now attended Pleasant Community Church. He sang in the choir, greeted people at the door and helped out with building construction issues.

"Just in time," he announced in his booming voice. "I'm not sure if anyone in this house is okay and at least two of them are crying."

"Cadence and Charlie?" she asked as she followed him inside the massive two-story foyer.

Ethan's mouth quirked as he looked down at her. "No, Charlie is fine. She's playing pool and having the time of her life torturing my brother. Cadence is in the bathroom. The door is locked and she won't open it."

"Charlie won't help?"

"Nope. She refuses. I think it's bothering her a bit, though. She's smiling, but every now and then I catch her glancing through the house, as if she's rethinking her stand. I admire the kid. If you're going to choose your battle, fight until the bitter end."

"Not helpful," Emery told him.

"Probably not," he agreed as he led her through the house, and then down a short hallway.

At the end of that hall, Beau stood with his forehead pressed against the door, a hand on the doorknob. "Cadence, please unlock the door."

He looked exhausted, unwell, beaten down.

Her heart tugged, requiring her to feel, and she didn't want to, not for him.

"I brought reinforcements," Ethan spoke in a quieter than normal tone.

"Thanks," Beau murmured, giving her a half grin, a look somewhere between relief and giving up.

Emery and Zeb joined him at the door. Zeb gave a scratch at the barricade.

Glancing down at her, Beau said, "I'm glad you're here."

"We'll get her out, I promise," she said, touching his arm briefly.

Ethan had left them. She heard the low murmur of his voice and then the strike of a cue against pool balls.

"Any suggestions?" Beau asked.

"Cadence, it's Em and Zeb. Zeb needs his ears scratched. He's very nervous in new places with new people. He wonders if you feel the same way, like maybe you need a friend?"

Silence.

He started to reach for the knob. She moved her hand to his, stopping him. She put a finger to her lips and cupped her ear, encouraging him to listen.

Zeb scratched again.

The lock clicked. Slowly, an inch at a time, the door opened. Cadence peered up at her with a tearstained face. It took Emery a painful moment, but she lowered herself to eye level with the child.

"I'm sorry," Emery said, leaning close. Zeb scooted in next to Cadence and the little girl wrapped her arms around the dog.

Cadence's hair was wet, her clothes clean but slightly damp. She hadn't used a towel, or at least hadn't used it well.

"Oh, munchkin," Emery soothed as she opened her arms and pulled the little girl close.

She heard a rustle as Beau moved closer and then he was at her side, not touching the child but putting himself in their circle. His profile was lean, his dark eyes concerned. The boy of her youth had become a man. People grew up. Her heart wanted to give him a chance, not for herself but for the two girls who needed him to be the man who would give them a home.

"I promise to do my best," he told Cadence in a somber voice as his gaze sought Emery's. "I'm going to make mistakes, so it will take the three of us working together."

Cadence buried her face in Zeb's neck. The dog leaned closer to the child. His ears perked, as if she was whispering something they couldn't hear.

"Would you like Nan's lasagna?" Emery asked Cadence as the girl cuddled the dog, who had made himself at home, sprawling out on the floor so that Cadence could crawl in next to him.

"I would!" Beau answered with enthusiasm.

His reply brought a lighter emotion to the moment. Emery made eye contact with Cadence, waggling her brows at the girl.

"I think Beau would eat worms if we told him Nan made them."

A surprising giggle escaped Cadence, but then her expression grew somber, as if she couldn't allow herself to be happy.

"Let's go," she told the child. She reached for the door frame, preparing herself for the awkward and sometimes painful act of standing— a shattered leg the only gift her father had ever given her. A hand clasped her forearm, causing a tremor that often happened at unfamiliar touch.

"Together," he said.

No, she told herself, not together. But he knew just the way to bring her to her feet in a fluid and almost painless way, placing the crutch in her hand afterward. Her heart squeezed painfully at his nearness and at the kindness of his gesture.

Zeb had gotten to his feet and Cadence had hold of his harness, her little hand holding tight to the dog. Zeb gave Emery a look with chocolate-brown eyes seeking permission to accompany his young friend. Emery handed the leash to Cadence.

"He's a pretty astonishing animal," Beau said as the four of them walked to the kitchen.

"He is," she agreed.

"I don't know how to do this," he admitted in a quiet voice strained with emotion.

What was she supposed to say to that? "You'll learn."

"Thank you for coming over."

Again, what should she say? She'd come for the girls, not for him. She didn't know how to banter with this man who had wounded her with his bullying.

"I put the lasagna in the oven," Ethan said as they entered the kitchen. "And Charlie is going to help make a salad."

"How did you get her to help?" Beau asked.

At the question, Ethan grinned. "I beat her in a few games of pool. Best two out of three gets to ask a favor of the other person. Anyway, I have to go. I'm team roping with Tucker and we're taking our horses down to the rodeo grounds to see how they work. See you all later. And I wish you the best."

With a wink, he tugged on a white cowboy hat and headed for the garage.

Charlie joined them in the kitchen. "Where's Nan?"

"She's having dinner with friends," Emery said. "But when she left, she gave me a message for you."

"What?"

Emery hugged the girl tight. "Nan said to remind you that you're loved and that you are fearfully and wonderfully made."

Charlie squirmed out of Emery's embrace. "Whatever. Did she send us food?"

"She did. And because you couldn't be kind or helpful, you're not only going to make a salad, you're also going to do the dishes."

"Fine," the teen huffed.

"Charlie," Emery called out to her retreating back as Charlie walked away from them.

"What?" Charlie paused, but she didn't turn to look back.

"I love you. I know you're hurting, but you can't mistreat the people in your life."

Charlie nodded, but she didn't turn. Emery guessed she was crying and wanted to hide her tears.

"How am I going to do this?" Beau asked, as if she had answers.

"You'll figure them out." She opened the double doors of the massive fridge and started pulling out salad items. She found a cheese stick and handed it over to Cadence. "This will hold you over until dinner."

"How long will the lasagna bake?" Beau asked as he helped Cadence open the cheese.

"Another thirty minutes. Charlie knows how to make a salad, so don't let her con you into making it." She found oven mitts. "You'll need these."

"You're not staying?" he asked, sounding truly shocked.

"I'm not staying. This is something you have to do, Beau. I know it isn't easy, but it will get easier. I can't…" She hesitated, then didn't finish. She couldn't be the person he relied on.

She picked up the leash that Cadence had dropped. Zeb left the child's side to return to hers.

"Thank you," Beau said. He started to follow her.

"You stay. I'll find my own way out."

She made it through the front door and then Charlie came running after her. "No! You can't go. You can't leave us like this."

The girl tackled her from behind. Emery lost her balance and they both fell to the porch. Charlie's arms were around her neck and she sobbed as she held on to her tight. Emery moved, sitting up as best she could. Zeb crawled into the middle of the heap.

"You can't go," Charlie said. "I know I'm bad. I know I shouldn't do the things I do, but I can't lose you, too."

Emery gathered the girl close. "Oh, honey, you haven't lost me. I'm right here."

Beau stepped out the door, hesitating when he spotted them on the porch together.

"I'll stay for dinner," Emery said as she met his troubled gaze.

Cadence joined them. She sat on Emery's lap and smoothed her sister's dark hair as the sobs quieted to an occasional hiccup. And then there were five of them as Beau lowered himself to sit on the other side of Charlie. Zeb shoved close to Charlie's face as he tried to give her comfort.

Emery prayed they would find a way through this disaster of a situation. She prayed for Beau, that he would be the father the girls needed. She prayed for herself, that she would know how best to help them—and how to let them go. As she prayed, she knew that God had brought her here because He had known the girls would need her.

But how could she help them when it meant being here with Beau Wilde?

Chapter Three

They sat on the porch together until the alarm beeped on Beau's watch. He'd set a timer to let him know when the lasagna would be ready. He didn't know if they were ready, though. Charlie remained curled against Emery's side. Cadence appeared to be dozing in her arms. Zeb had moved so that he wasn't on top of them. Instead, he remained watchful at Charlie's feet.

Beau noticed Emery grimace, then she shifted.

"We should get up," he suggested. "The lasagna will be done and we still need to make that salad."

Charlie sniffled and wiped the hair from her eyes. "I'll make the salad."

"Are you sure?" Beau asked, cautious because the girl, and the moment, seemed fragile.

"I'm sure," she told him, the wariness in her

expression letting him know that they weren't exactly allies. Not yet.

In time, maybe they would regain their footing. She would remember him as the man who filled the role of uncle in her life and stop thinking of him as the enemy. The teen clambered to her feet and leaned over to pull Cadence from Emery's lap. "I'll put her on the couch," she said as she carried Cadence back into the house with a brief backward glance at them. She gave him a look, then nodded toward Emery, sending a silent message. And then she was gone, letting the door close softly behind her.

Zeb stood at the closed door and whined. He glanced back at his mistress and then at the door before returning to Emery. He nuzzled her arm. Her eyes were closed and one tear sneaked out, trickling down her cheek.

Beau pushed to his feet. "Emery, are you okay?"

She shook her head. "No. I'm not. My heart is breaking for them. And even for you. Those men…" She briefly covered her face with her hands. "They stole the futures those girls might have had. For what? A car? Some money? Why?"

He found himself at a loss as he processed her words. He knew the story. He'd read the police reports. He'd talked to lawyers. Hearing it from her, as she looked up at him, eyes ravaged with the heartache of the situation, it gutted him.

"I know," he said simply. "I don't have answers."

She struggled to her feet, using the wall and her crutch to gain her footing, his help unnecessary.

"Do you have any suggestions?"

"I wish I did."

"Me, too." He stared into her stormy gray eyes. "I know you have many reasons to doubt me, but can we call a truce? For the girls."

"A truce?" She took a careful step back, putting several feet between them. Dusk had fallen and he could hear the tree frogs beginning their song of spring. Somewhere in the distance a coyote howled.

It sounded like the music of any other peaceful country evening. His heart played a different tune. There on the porch of his childhood home, his heart waited, praying she would give him a chance.

"A truce," he repeated, needing this more than he could put into words. "I know I hurt you in the past. I'd like to show you I'm no longer that person. For the girls. For you."

"And?" she said, prodding him to admit his fears.

"I can't do this alone. I need your help."

"Why me?" she asked, sounding unsure, and yet maybe, just maybe, she sounded like she might be willing. "I'm sure there are other people in your life you can call on to help you."

"My mom is recovering from open-heart surgery. The doctor refuses to let her travel or she would have been here. It's clear that the girls trust you. It's you they need right now."

"I'd do anything for those girls, but I'm not sure if I can do this…with you."

"Two weeks, Emery." He wouldn't resort to pleading, but he was pretty close. "All we need is two weeks to help them—to help us—adjust. Maybe in those two weeks you'll accept that I'm a better man than I was a boy."

He needed her approval. In a matter of hours, that had become very important to him for reasons he hadn't yet figured out.

With her hand on the door, she hesitated. "I'll consider it. For the girls."

"Okay." He felt alarmingly untethered. By her? He couldn't say for sure, but he did know that she mattered in this situation.

"For now, I'll stay and help you get them settled."

"Thank you," he said as he reached for the door.

As it opened, he spotted Charlie sliding around the corner of the foyer into the kitchen.

At the suspicious sight, Emery laughed. The tension between them evaporated.

"I imagine she must have been a funny, loved and smart girl." Emery didn't have to say "before." He knew. They knew.

"She was." He paused in the foyer. "I spoke to Garret right before I left for Africa on the mission trip. We were going to get together this summer and have an overnight float trip down the river. Dana and the girls were going to meet us at the halfway point."

He closed his eyes at the rush of emotion the memory brought. Her hand touched his arm, then lingered for a moment. "I'm sorry. I know he was your friend. We've all been focused on the girls, but…" She shrugged. "I know it isn't easy."

"Yeah," he spoke, and his voice didn't sound as if it belonged to him. "It isn't."

"The lasagna is ready," Charlie called out from the kitchen, her voice a little too chipper. "I made the salad."

She'd done more than that. She'd set the table and poured everyone drinks. Beau gave an approving nod as he lifted Cadence off a stool at the kitchen island.

"Dinnertime," he told her as he held her close. She rested her head on his shoulder. That gesture felt like a place to begin.

He settled her in a chair, then pulled out a chair for Charlie and one for Emery. Charlie scooted in immediately, claiming the seat next to her sister.

Emery hesitated, her gaze lingering on each of them for a moment before taking her seat.

"I'd like to pray," Beau said, and from the looks on the faces of the three females at the table, that must have been a surprising statement coming from him.

Charlie let go of the salad tongs in her hand. "Oh, sure, okay. We never did that at home."

"You were used to praying at Nan's," Emery reminded her.

"Yeah, but I thought it was something just Nan did." Charlie sat back in her chair and positioned her hands in front of her face.

"I'd like for us to hold hands," Beau told them.

Charlie opened one eye. "Now you're pushing it."

He chuckled. "I'm sorry, but I think this is important. It's our first meal together." As a family.

He didn't add those words. The girls had lost the only family that mattered and the three of them certainly didn't feel like family.

They joined hands and he prayed for the blessing of a meal to eat, for the blessing of peace.

He prayed for each of them to find strength in faith. He prayed he would be led by wisdom.

Together they ate that first meal and it helped that Emery stayed. She kept the conversation going, talking about school, church and other activities the girls had taken part in.

Beau studied Charlie with her chopped-off hair and oversize sweatshirt, her eyes a mixture of sad and angry, but a remnant of the girl he'd known still remained. He prayed they would be able to help her be that girl again.

And Cadence looked so much like Garret that it hurt, with her strawberry blond curls. He prayed they would find a way to unlock her silence and return her to the chatterbox he'd enjoyed carting around on his shoulders when he visited his friends.

His gaze shifted to study Emery as she picked at her food while making small talk with Charlie. He was overwhelmed with the need to have her as a friend.

He found himself intrigued by the woman she'd become.

A woman who, even though she wanted nothing to do with him, had stayed to help them through this first very difficult night.

Emery Guthrie was too good for him. She'd probably always been too good for him. That much was clear.

* * *

After dinner, Emery stayed to help the girls settle into their new room on the second floor of the home. It was a pretty room decorated in white and pale blue. Sheer white curtains covered the windows and next to the window sat a white rocking chair. A soft blue rug warmed the hardwood floors.

The girls had only brought clothing and other necessities from Nan's. The rest of their belongings would be delivered in the coming days. For tonight, they had their favorite pajamas, stuffed animals and toiletries. They had each brought the small personal quilts that Nan had made for them.

As they unpacked, Cadence climbed up on the bed and wrapped herself in her quilt, as if wrapping herself in Nan's comforting arms. Emery remembered nights as a teen when she'd done the same. She remembered a night when she'd wanted her quilt so terribly that it had hurt, but she hadn't been allowed to have it.

Those weren't the memories for this night. Tonight, the girls needed for her to distract them, to keep them thinking about something other than their heartache and the changes taking place in their lives.

"How many goats do you have?" Emery asked Beau.

He moved away from the door where he'd been standing, watching. "I'm not really sure. They're Ethan's. A few, I think."

"I bet the girls will love meeting them," she said, hoping he'd keep the conversation going.

He took a seat in the rocking chair near the window. "I think we can arrange that. It's hard to tell what all Ethan has out there. He brings home strays. Last year it was a llama."

"Kittens?" Emery asked, smiling down at Cadence, who moved to the end of the bed where she sat and crawled up into her lap, still wrapped in the quilt.

"There are always kittens around," Beau said, giving her a smile.

She tried to ignore the softness of his expression and the way it started to undo the anger and hurt inside her.

"We have to brush our teeth," Charlie said as she shoved the last of her clothes in a drawer. She shot Emery a mutinous look and grabbed the small overnight bag with their toiletries. "And we don't like kittens."

Cadence made a tiny sound of protest.

"Sounds like we do like kittens," Emery countered.

Charlie took Cadence by the hand. "Let's brush our teeth."

Cadence let go of her quilt and followed her

older sister to the bathroom across the hall. Emery started to stand, but Beau put a hand out, stopping her.

"I've got this."

She wanted to argue, but instead she let him go. He needed this time with the girls. And she needed to sit for a moment and gather herself, gather her strength and her runaway emotions. Long ago she'd realized that her superpower wasn't in trying to do everything that everyone else did. It was in accepting her limitations and doing what she could to the best of her ability.

As the girls finished their nighttime routine, Emery pulled down the blankets on the bed. After they were done in the bathroom, the girls crossed the hall together and climbed in, cuddling close as they'd been doing nightly at Nan's. Cadence burrowed into her sister, reaching for her quilt, pulling it close to her face. Charlie wrapped comforting arms around her sister and held her close.

That was a lot of pressure for an older sibling. Charlie had to be the security for Cadence, the familiar presence. Emery pulled the blankets over them, then sat on the edge of the bed. Beau moved back to the rocking chair and sat with his long legs crossed at the ankles. He leaned slightly forward, watching with thoughtful eyes.

"Do you want me to rub your back?" Emery

asked Cadence. The child nodded as her thumb went to her mouth.

"Don't suck your—" Charlie started.

Emery cut her off with a shake of her head. This wasn't the night to worry about breaking bad habits. This was hard enough without taking away something that might help Cadence feel safe. But what about Charlie? What made Charlie feel safe?

As Emery rubbed Cadence's back, she sang to the girls. Charlie might act tough, but she loved their bedtime song and prayers. Sometimes, she even allowed Emery to comfort her. Sometimes.

"Do you want to pray?" Emery asked Beau.

He'd been sitting silently. Her back was to him, but she knew he was watching, taking in the routine, hopefully remembering so that he could continue the steps that helped the girls feel more at peace.

"Of course I'll pray," he said.

They closed their eyes and she waited. His voice was low and comforting as he prayed for them to have a good night's sleep, to feel safe and secure, and to know that God was with them, giving them peace, healing their hearts.

"Where was God that night?" Charlie whispered, her arm tossed over her eyes, covering the expression that would have ravaged Emery's heart.

"Sheltering you," Emery said.

"He could have saved…"

Emery's breath shuddered on the exhale. "Oh, sweet girl."

She put a hand on Charlie's shoulder. "We can't understand why things happen the way they do. It hurts and it doesn't make sense, but we have to know that as time goes by, it will hurt less."

"When?" Charlie asked, her voice wobbling as she lost the fight to stay strong.

"It will take time, but allow yourself to laugh when you feel like laughing. Allow yourself to have fun. Also, let yourself remember the good times you all had together."

Charlie shook her head. "I don't want to remember."

"In time you will."

Charlie snuggled close to her sister, brushing off Emery's hand. The younger girl had fallen asleep and Charlie tucked her strawberry blond head under her chin. She sighed and closed her eyes.

Emery didn't move.

"You can go." Charlie opened her eyes. "We're going to be fine."

Emery leaned in to kiss her forehead. "I'm just a phone call away."

"Until we leave for Tulsa," Charlie accused. As if Emery had any control over this whole situation.

"Even then, you can call." Emery smoothed a hand over Charlie's head, slowly, hoping the girl would relax. "Sleep, Charlie."

Charlie settled into the pillow and squeezed her eyes closed. Emery remained, still running her hand over the dyed hair that they'd tried very hard to fix. Eventually Charlie's breathing slowed.

Emery waited a few more minutes, then got up from the bed. Zeb had been sleeping on the rug. He stood, stretched and then nuzzled her hand in his comforting way. He truly was her best friend. She switched his leash to her right hand and grabbed the ever-present crutch. With a quick look to Beau, she left the room. He followed, but she knew from his steps that he hesitated, probably at the bed.

She went on, because it would take her more time to navigate the steps. She'd made it halfway down when he caught up with her. He didn't speak. Instead, he adjusted his speed and remained at her side.

Silence hung between them, but it wasn't the

uncomfortable variety that she would have expected.

"Would you like a cup of coffee or tea before
you leave?" he asked as they walked through
the house.

"I think I should go," she told him, stopping
briefly in the doorway that led from the small
dining nook to the foyer. It would be easy to sit
here in this calm and inviting space and have a
cup of tea. It would be easy, she realized, to sit
with him and share a moment of quiet. Too easy.

"I understand," he said. "I appreciate your
help tonight. I know you did it for them, not for
me, but I'm glad you were here."

"So am I." She realized as she said it that she
meant it.

He rubbed a hand across his eyes. "This is
a mess."

"It is," she agreed. "They're sweet girls. Even
Charlie. Remember that when she tests your
limits."

He smiled at that, and she saw the man he'd
become, not the boy he'd been. This man had
fine lines at the corners of his eyes. He had a
five-o'clock shadow on his lean cheeks. He'd
lost the swagger of youth and there was a hu-
mility in his expression, probably earned from
his current situation.

She drew back from those thoughts because

trust wasn't earned from a smile or a hurt look. The wounds he'd inflicted on her went deep.

"Good night," she told him, fully intending to depart and let him live his life as it now stood. No looking back.

She started her slow journey to the front door, feeling every step because it had been a long day. She was tired, hurting and... Her heart ached as if it had been physically injured.

He followed her. Remaining with her as she eased her way off the porch and across the lawn to her car. With each step, she wished more than ever that she had taken this walk alone.

Alone she might have stopped to cry. Alone she could have taken her time, caught her breath, said a prayer for the girls, for herself and even for Beau.

His presence was a little bit overwhelming.

"Thank you," she said as she opened her car door. She motioned and Zeb jumped inside.

Headlights flashed and then dimmed. Ethan had returned. The horse trailer attached to the back of the truck rattled as he drove down the driveway.

"Emery, I am sincerely sorry for the way I treated you in the past. And I am truly thankful for your help tonight."

"I would say 'anytime,' but I'm afraid that

would mean a daily drive out here to rescue you."

"Is that humor?" he asked.

"It is. I do joke from time to time."

"I like that," he said. "It would be good if this wasn't a goodbye. I think the girls need you. I definitely need your help."

She wanted to tell him no, definitely not. She wanted to get in her car, drive away and never see Beau Wilde again. If not for the girls, she would have done just that. But the girls needed continuity. They needed people they were familiar with. They needed help adjusting to their very difficult loss.

"I'll be around, Beau. If you need me or Nan, we'll be here." For the time being, that was all she could give him.

"Thank you."

"Don't forget about school tomorrow. Eight a.m. sharp." She noticed a tremor in his hand as it rested on the car door. A flutter of concern for him took her by surprise. "You should go inside and rest. You're going to need it."

"I should," he agreed.

He started to walk away.

"Are you okay?" she called out.

He hesitated.

"I will be." He kept walking.

Emery got in her car, watching as he made his

slow way back to the house. She was surprised when he seemed to need to hold the railing to make it up the few steps to the porch.

"Time to go home, Zeb." She gave her trusty friend a pat on the head as she backed out of the drive. A quick look at the house and she saw that he was still there, standing under the soft light of the porch.

As much as she wanted to not care, she did. She cared, she told herself, because he mattered to Cadence and Charlie. His health mattered to those two girls. It mattered if he was good, if he was kind.

For the girls, not for her.

For her, he was no longer the monster under her bed. His torture of her had been an unfinished book, a story without an ending. Now he was an adult with a life that had, overnight, become more complicated than he'd ever imagined. A life that would briefly, very briefly, be connected to her own.

Chapter Four

Her father stood over her, the ever-present baseball bat in his meaty fists. He was a monster with bloodshot eyes and stringy brown hair. Emery cowered as he swung the bat, hitting her leg once, twice, three times. The pain, so intense she felt sick, radiated from her foot to her back. She tried to escape, but no matter where she tried to turn, he was there. His face distorted, changed and became… Beau Wilde.

She was dreaming. She forced herself to swim to the surface of sleep, pushing the dream away as she did. In wakefulness she realized, although her legs felt heavy and weighted down, she could move.

It was Zeb who had her trapped. He was sprawled across her like a labradoodle comforter. He eyed her with that solemn look of his and then belly crawled to her side, where he rested his chin on her shoulder.

"I'm fine," she whispered into the darkness of early morning. She glanced at her watch. It was just after seven and it was Saturday. She could have slept in. She'd really wanted to. This past week had drained her. Not only the situation with Beau and the girls, but also the final countdown at school. Everyone was getting a little stressed as they neared the final days of the school year.

Zeb pushed at her with his cold doggy nose. She ruffled his ears and he fairly moaned his happiness. "You're spoiled."

She leaned back on the pillow and closed her eyes. "I could sleep for thirty more minutes."

If her heart hadn't been beating so hard. If the dream hadn't left her battling memories of the past. Also, if she didn't have to go tend to the community garden that she'd started as a way for teens to help give back. It was especially effective for those who had been in trouble. It taught them how to work together and how to take pride in a job well-done. At least that was her hope.

"Let's go, Zeb. Time to rise and shine." At her announcement, the dog covered his face with a paw.

A short time later she descended the stairs, Zeb following at her heels.

The light was on over the kitchen sink and there was coffee in the carafe next to the pot. She poured herself a mug, added a little cream from the pitcher and headed out the back door to find Nan.

Nan made custom river johnboats. For years the business had prospered and she'd supported herself and all of the girls she'd raised. She'd kept hoping one of her girls would take over and make the business their own.

In the past couple of years, several of the girls had come home. Avery was first. She'd returned to Pleasant with her daughter Quinn. Quinn's father, Grayson Stone, had arrived at nearly the same time. They were a family now, Grayson, Avery and Quinn, along with a new baby girl, Alexis.

Clara had returned next, expecting a baby and looking for a place to heal. She'd found Tucker Church and now the two were married and parents of sweet baby Grace. Clara helped Tucker run his river outfitter business, but she came by from time to time to work in Nan's boat shop.

Emery entered the shop, breathing in deep of the smells that always comforted. Wood, varnish, paint and coffee scented the workshop air. Nan moved quietly about the space, putting together equipment and whatever she might need to start her day. A half-finished johnboat, sanded but not yet stained, the seats not yet in place, sat on the racks Nan used to keep the boat off the ground. The boat would be a sixteen-foot masterpiece, every detail handcrafted and perfected by Nan. She would lovingly sand the wood, put the pieces together, install live wells for fish, cup holders, dry storage—whatever the client might want in their new riverboat. Each boat Nan made was unique.

"Good morning." Nan waved as she continued to work, goggles covering her eyes. "Do you have plans today?"

"I do. I'm working in the community garden."

"I wondered about where you were last night. Did you go out on a date?" Nan asked. The question seemed more suited to one of the other girls Nan had raised. Emery didn't date much. Dating had never worked out for her. Men were sometimes embarrassed by her crutch, sometimes put off by her seriousness, and sometimes she backed away because she didn't want to be hurt.

Last night she'd been home. She guessed that Nan meant Thursday evening.

"No, I was here."

Nan frowned a little. "That's right, and you were with Beau the night before. Helping with the girls. I worry about this situation, Emery. A man raising two young girls on his own."

Emery took a seat next to Nan. "It won't be easy for him."

Nan gave her a long look. "It was good of you to help him."

Nan meant because of the past. Emery didn't know how to respond.

For a while they sat in silence as Nan worked on installing a wooden seat at the back of the boat. After some time, Nan looked up, her expression troubled.

"You didn't sleep good," Nan said. "I heard you cry out during the night."

"I'm so sorry. Did I wake you?"

"Land sakes, no. I was up. I almost came in and woke you, but I didn't know if that would help."

"I'm fine," she said after taking a sip of coffee. She could have said more, about Beau Wilde being in Pleasant and dredging up the past. Instead, she took another sip of her coffee and worked on letting go.

Nan studied her face. "I know you don't want to hear this, but I think having Beau around is important. You've forgiven him, but forgiving him face-to-face, that takes a little more work."

"I love you, Nan."

"Is that your way of telling me I'm right?" Nan winked at her, then she went back to work.

"You're always right." She kissed her foster mom—her adoptive mom—on the cheek. "I'll call you later."

"To check up on me?" Nan said with a sheen of tears in her eyes.

"Nope, to tell you how my day is going."

"You've never been very good at fibbing," Nan said. "If it makes you feel better, you can check on me later."

"Nan, I..." Emery didn't know what she'd planned to say. There were so many thoughts, so many feelings. Losing Nan this way. Watching Charlie and Cadence struggle through their loss. All of it felt insurmountable. She knew it wasn't, but at the moment it felt like the darkest storm of her life.

The struggles they all faced put the small things in perspective. Beau was one of the smaller, more temporary problems.

"Stop looking at me like that," Nan warned, wagging her finger as she did.

Emery found a smile. "Okay. On my way home I'm going to get brownies. Doesn't that sound good?"

Nan waved her out the door. "Yes, bring brownies."

She blew Nan a kiss and she left, pretending it didn't hurt and that this day was like any other.

When Emery pulled up to the community garden, which was located on a patch of land near the community church's youth building, Pastor Matthews was waiting for her. He waved a spade and motioned to the teens already at work.

Emery and Zeb joined him and she couldn't help but feel better about life. Pastor Matthews had that effect on people. He had a joy and optimism that overlooked all obstacles.

"A few of your kids showed up early," he explained as he walked over to her. "I was here working on my sermon, tilling up a bit more ground. So I put your kids to work planting carrot seeds and watering. We're going to be doing a lot of watering if we don't get rain soon. May is the wrong time of year to be dry."

"I agree and I'm not a fan of watering." She leaned on her crutch and watched the few students who had shown up early. Alex, Tom and Lila. Good kids who just had a difficult time understanding the reason for rules. "Thank you for helping us with this project, Pastor."

"My pleasure," he said in his somewhat booming pastor voice. "I think this garden will benefit the youth and those who will receive the bounty of their work."

"That's my plan." She watched as Alex tossed a handful of weeds. Of course, the dirt hit Tom in the face. "No more of that, please!"

Alex turned, wide-eyed at being caught.

"Oh, sorry. I didn't see you there." Alex could at least look apologetic. The corner of Emery's mouth tugged upward at the contrite look on the teen's face.

"That isn't the issue. Whether I'm here to see or not, you should make the right choice."

The boys both saluted and went back to work.

"You don't have Cadence and Charlie?" Pastor Matthews observed.

"Beau Wilde took custody of them the day before yesterday."

"How did it go?"

"It wasn't easy. I went to the ranch and helped them get settled."

"I'm glad. This is a difficult situation all around. I'm glad Mr. Wilde has you to help with the transition."

Emery focused on the students who were, at the moment, dragging a water hose toward the garden.

"I should oversee this," she told Pastor Matthews. "Or we won't have a garden left."

Also, she didn't want to talk about Beau

Wilde, Cadence or Charlie. Her heart ached for the girls, for the way their lives had been ripped apart and their family destroyed.

"And I should finish my sermon for tomorrow," Pastor Matthews said with a wide grin. "I'm sure it will be well received. The members always love a rousing sermon on the importance of giving."

"I know they do," she said as she watched Alex turn the hose on the other kids and not the garden.

"Emery, if you ever need to talk, my door is always open."

Emery saw the concern in his eyes and forced herself to relax. "I appreciate that, Pastor. But I'm fine. Really."

"I know you'll be fine, but I also know this has been a difficult situation." His hand rested briefly on her shoulder.

After he left, Zeb nudged at her hand. "I know you're here," she told the dog.

"Stop wasting water," she called out to the kids. Alex immediately began to water the tomato plants. "I'm glad you're here so early today."

The teen had been late the previous week.

"Mr. Stanford said I have to be on time." Alex moved the water hose over to the zucchini plants. "You think we'll really get vegetables?"

"I know we will," she assured him.

"Uh-oh," Alex muttered. "There's Stanford."

"*Mr.* Stanford," she reminded. "We show respect to our elders."

"Right. I'm sorry." Alex moved on to the next row of plants while the other teens worked on evening the ground that the pastor had recently tilled but needed to be raked out smooth.

Emery moved away from the group, allowing Zeb to stay with the students. He especially liked Lila, and the girl with her purple-and-black hair liked Zeb. She scratched his ears and told him secrets that would probably break the heart of any non-canine.

"Miss Guthrie," Louis Stanford, the county juvenile officer, greeted as he drew closer.

"Mr. Stanford." She smiled at the man who had recently told her he was looking forward to retiring in the next few years. He looked forward to buying one of Nan's boats and spending a lot of time on the river. He dabbed at perspiration that beaded across his forehead with a handkerchief from his pocket.

"I was hoping I would catch you here. I wanted to speak to you in private."

She glanced around. "This is probably as private as it gets. Is something wrong?"

He motioned her toward a nearby bench and she gladly took the offer to sit and talk. As they walked, Zeb glanced their way. He started to get up, but Lila said something and the dog remained at her side.

"Looks like the group is working well together," Louis said as they seated themselves beneath the shade of a giant oak.

"They're learning. That's what this project is all about, learning to work together toward something."

"It's a great idea." Louis took a deep breath in, mopping more sweat off his face. "I do wish it wasn't this hot in May."

"Same," she agreed. She doubted Louis wanted to discuss the weather.

"I won't keep you. I just wanted to tell you of a position that I thought might interest you. In light of your continued studies, you'll soon have that doctorate, will you not? That's a degree that goes beyond the needs of a school counselor."

"I like my job," she informed him. "I do want to someday call myself a psychologist, but truly, working with these kids, being able to guide them, to give them support, it's rewarding."

"What about a job in a residential home near St. Louis? Would you ever consider something like that?"

"Maybe someday," she told him. Someday looked to be further down the road. Home was where she needed to be, for herself, for Nan and for her family.

"I have a friend who is looking to fill a position in a facility, residential treatment. A rewarding, if tough, career. You have such a way with teens…"

She shook her head, stopping him. "Mr. Stanford, I can't leave Pleasant right now."

"Because of Nan," he said with a level of compassion that didn't surprise her. "I knew that would probably be your answer. I just wanted to give you the opportunity and time to think on it. They won't fill the position until the end of summer."

"I will think about it," she assured him. "I just don't think this is the right time for major changes."

"We never know what God has planned for us, do we?" He stood, brushed his dress slacks and stood for a moment watching the teens. "Alex giving you any problems?"

"None," she said.

"Never let your guard down, Miss Guthrie."

"I never do." Truer words were never spoken. Letting her guard down had gotten her hurt, physically and emotionally. She made a habit to always be vigilant.

Beau Wilde came to mind. He wasn't going to hurt her because she wouldn't let him. As she'd said, she never let her guard down with anyone other than her closest friends and family. Beau didn't fit inside that very small circle.

"If you want lunch at the café, we need to go," Beau told the teenager who seemed intent on ignoring him. She stood at the fence petting a pretty black filly and pretending she couldn't hear him.

"I don't think she's going," Ethan said as he walked out of the barn.

"Isn't Cadence with you?" Beau looked past his brother. Two days in and he couldn't say he was doing a bang-up job with the girls. The previous day they were almost an hour late for school. Then, after school, he'd momentarily lost Cadence.

"She was right behind me," Ethan said as he turned back toward the barn. "Oh, she found a kitten."

Sure enough, Cadence appeared in the doorway with a kitten. The gray ball of fluff was cuddled close as if it were the most precious thing ever.

Charlie glanced back, her hand still on the horse's neck. "She'll get scratched."

"She speaks," Ethan teased. He adjusted his black cowboy hat and studied the girl. "If you cooperate a little, I'll let you spend some time with that horse. She needs to be brushed, worked on a halter and lead rope, and she needs for someone to love on her a little."

Beau swung his gaze from Cadence to Charlie, wondering how the girl would take to the idea of working with the horse.

"Is that a bribe?" Charlie asked. "Do you think that'll make me want to do what you all ask me? Like that will make me okay with leaving Pleasant and going to Tulsa? We *aren't* a family. We won't *ever* be a family." She gave them her back.

"We can try our hardest..." The moment the words left Beau's mouth, he knew they were wrong. Charlie didn't want a replacement family. And he didn't blame her.

"Right, even you don't believe that. You're just trying to make me feel better. Well, guess what? I don't. So—"

There was a loud hiss, and Cadence screamed as the kitten clawed its way up her arm. Beau reached for the feline, holding it by the scruff of its neck as it fought to get away. Ethan's border collie jumped in circles, barking at the kitten. Cadence cried silent tears as blood dripped down her cheek.

"See what you've done! You don't even know how to take care of kids!" Charlie hurried to her little sister. "We need peroxide and bandages."

"Peroxide and bandages?" Beau looked at his brother.

"I doubt I have either of those things," Ethan admitted as he took the kitten from Beau. "I have some salve in the barn. I'll get it when I return the troublemaker back to the mama cat."

"Animal salve?" Charlie's eyes widened. "You've got to be kidding."

"Call Emery?" Ethan suggested.

The thought was tempting. "No, we can handle this," Beau said.

Charlie gave him a narrow-eyed look, obviously doubting his ability to handle anything. He picked Cadence up and examined the scratch.

"Does it hurt?" he asked the silent child.

She nodded but said nothing.

"Can we at least get a paper towel?" Charlie asked, as she examined the scratch. "But no animal salve."

"Sure thing," Ethan said. He headed for the barn, his long legs carrying him quickly.

"It's okay, Caddie. I'm here. I'm here." Charlie kissed her sister's cheek.

Beau watched the two together and, not for the first time, tried to imagine that fateful day they'd hidden together. The day that had changed their lives forever.

Charlie shot him a look, as if she knew where

his mind had gone. For a moment she looked much younger than fourteen.

Ethan returned with wet paper towels and Charlie snatched them from him. Beau started to take over, but something in Charlie's actions made him think that if she didn't care for her sister herself, she might fall apart.

Not surprisingly, she took Cadence from his arms and headed across the lawn in the direction of his truck. The two girls made a clear statement that they didn't need anyone else.

But they did. No matter how independent Charlie might act, she needed for him to be the adult.

"We should go," Beau said to the one left standing next to him, Ethan.

"You going to be okay?" his older brother asked.

"Yeah, I'm good. Maybe some ice cream at Tilly's will do the trick." He pulled his keys out of his pocket and started to walk away. "Will you be here when I get back?"

"Should be. I need to check that thirty acres near the highway and make sure the pond is still full. We need a real rain or I'm going to be hauling water."

"Yeah, rain would be good." Beau climbed in his truck and closed the door. Rain was the last thing on his mind, but small talk helped clear his thoughts.

As they pulled out of the drive, he glanced back at the girls. Cadence seemed to have recovered. But Charlie looked pretty ragged. Her eyes were red and overflowing with tears that she quickly blinked away.

"It wasn't your fault, Charlie," he told her. She glanced his way, unsure. "The kitten. It wasn't your fault."

"We were still there because of me," she said, looking stricken. He wondered at that look. Were they still talking about the kitten? Or was this about something else?

"You're right," he agreed, and he sure hoped he was saying the right thing. "But Cadence picking up that kitten had nothing to do with you."

"If I'd listened and we'd left when you said to leave…" She let the words trail off.

Beau glanced in the rearview mirror. She looked out the window at passing scenery, but her hand wiped away a stream of tears rolling down her cheeks. He needed help. Though he was generally an independent guy, he could admit he was in over his head. He could also admit that the person he needed was Emery Guthrie.

The woman least likely to want to spend time

with him. And for good reason. Plus, he wasn't used to a woman who really didn't want anything to do with him.

Fortunately, the woman in question happened to be in town. As they drove in on the back roads, he passed by the community church and saw her there in a garden, working with a group of teens.

He pulled in, not really thinking it through but knowing they probably all needed her presence.

As they got out of the truck, Charlie shot him a questioning look. "Why are we here?"

"I thought we could say hi before we go to lunch," he explained.

"Right," the teen said. "We both know that isn't true."

They walked together the short distance to the garden. Emery was talking to a tall, bulky kid.

Cadence broke loose and ran over to Emery.

"Hey," Emery said as little arms went around her waist. She hugged Cadence but immediately focused in on Charlie. And then she turned that startling gray gaze on him.

"We wanted to say hi." He sounded awkward. That wasn't something he was used to feeling around women.

"What happened here?" She moved the paper

towel that Cadence was still holding to the wound.

"Cat scratch," he explained.

"I have a first aid kit in my car, with bandages."

First aid kit. Why hadn't he thought of that? Charlie wandered away, drawn by the garden and the other teens.

"Is she okay?" Emery asked when the girl had moved out of earshot.

"It's all good. Just some emotions about leaving Pleasant in two weeks."

Emery looked down at Cadence, who now had her arms wrapped around Zeb, her mouth close to his ear, as if she was telling him her secrets.

Together the two of them walked a short distance away from the adults.

"Sorry, that's not true," Beau admitted. "Charlie is beating herself up because Cadence got hurt. She thinks if she'd listened to me and if we'd left on time, this wouldn't have happened. It's a lot of guilt over a cat scratch."

"I'd tell her therapist about it," Emery suggested in that soft voice of hers. She had a way about her, a way of making him feel grounded, as if he wasn't in this alone.

He couldn't help but be thankful that she was

here in town. He couldn't help but want to keep her in their lives just a little bit longer.

For the girls, obviously. Anything else would be out of the question. He'd just inherited two very troubled children and his focus needed to be on them.

Right?

Chapter Five

Emery needed a moment away from Beau, a moment to gather her thoughts and maybe some courage. She also needed to give attention to the students who had stopped gardening and were starting to pick up the tools that they kept in the church toolshed. "I need to talk to the kids before they leave," she said, still distracted by Beau, by his nearness, by Charlie and Cadence. "We've been here almost two hours and it looks as if they're ready to go." A couple of students had already been picked up by parents.

"Don't let us stop you," Beau said. "Is there anything we can do to help?"

She shook her head at the offer.

"Are we finished for the day?" she asked as Alex grabbed the water hose and started to roll it up.

"Yeah," the boy answered. "My dad is still

pretty mad that I'm in trouble. He said if I work past noon…"

Alex stopped talking and glanced away, his expression shuttered. "Anyway, I have to go."

"Do you need a ride?"

"Nope. I can walk. Lila and Tom are walking with me. We all live in the same area."

"Gotcha. Don't forget to grab a sandwich from the cooler."

"Will do," Alex assured her as he headed for the cooler. She guessed the boy was a bottomless pit when it came to food.

When she turned back to Beau, he was standing a short distance away with the girls. Cadence and Charlie sat on the ground with Zeb. The dog was sprawled out, enjoying the extra attention. Beau brushed a hand over his cheek as he watched them. She felt for him, for the situation he'd found himself in with the girls. She felt for him because he'd lost his best friend.

He looked exhausted and a little bit lost in his new role of guardian. He also didn't look completely healthy.

Charlie clambered to her feet. Cadence and Zeb followed. They found a stick and the three moved a short distance away. Zeb loved to play fetch.

"She's so angry," he said as he watched the girls play with Zeb. From the distance he heard

Charlie's constant chattering with her younger sister, as if trying to get her to talk.

"Their therapist is trying to help her with that. Mrs. Graves is teaching her ways to process all of the emotions she's dealing with, but it's going to take some time."

"She doesn't want to leave here," he said, looking up at the sky and drawing in a deep breath. "But I don't know what other options we have."

"Give them time," Emery encouraged. "Give yourself time."

Emery's phone buzzed. She pulled it from her pocket and answered.

"Hey, Avery, what's up?" She stepped a few feet away from him.

"I just got a call from Tilly," Avery started. "Nan is at the café and she's a little lost. We're in Springfield. And Clara and Tucker went down to pick up canoes in Arkansas." Avery paused. "I'm sorry, I know you're probably busy and I hate to bother you, but…"

"Why would you even say that?" Emery chided. "Of course I can go check on her."

"Okay. Call me later."

She ended the call.

"Is there something I can do?" Beau asked.

"Nan is at Tilly's and she's upset. I need to go check on her and possibly take her home."

"Is her car at Tilly's?" he asked.

"I'm sure it is."

"I can drive you over," he said, as if it was a given. "You can drive her home in her car. I'll follow and bring you back here."

The plan had merit. It was either that or leave Nan's car at the café. Accepting the plan meant accepting more time with Beau. Her gaze shot past him to where the girls played with Zeb. "Thank you," she said.

He gave her a tender look, one that said he cared. Her heart reacted, wanting to trust that look, trust that he could be a friend. Her heart also kept careful score of the number of times her trust had led to heartbreak.

"Are you okay?" he asked as he waved for the girls to join them.

"I'm fine."

"Of course you are," Beau said. "There's a safety in always telling others that you're fine."

She didn't appreciate that he could read her so easily.

The girls joined them and he explained the situation. Together the four of them, plus Zeb, walked to the parking lot.

They neared his big four-door Ford truck.

Why did men like trucks that you needed a ladder to get into?

"Problem?" he asked. Did he seem slightly out of breath?

"Not really. You okay?"

She waited for an answer because it was easier to focus on him than herself.

"I'm good."

She arched a brow at the obvious untruth.

"I'm recovering," he amended with a flash of white teeth and dimples. "So, about the look you just gave my truck…"

"I just wondered why it had to be so tall," she admitted, feeling heat climb into her cheeks.

She grabbed the handle on the inside of the truck door and managed the awkward and embarrassing act of climbing up.

"I'll get a step stool for next time."

"I'm going to hold you to that," she said after gaining the seat.

This felt like flirting. She never flirted. Ever.

They drove the short distance to Tilly's Café. The small-town diner was always packed for lunch.

"I'm not ready for this," she confided as they walked up the sidewalk.

"For?" he prodded.

"For losing her," she admitted out loud for the first time. "I know that because of this horrible illness, we will lose her. She'll be with us in body, for a time, but she won't really be with us."

"I understand. We lost my grandfather to Alzheimer's. That's the reason my parents moved to St. Louis, to be with my grandmother now that she's alone."

"I'm sorry," she told him. "It's hard, watching them struggle to remember things they've always known."

His hand briefly touched hers, a touch that took her by surprise. She'd always been a solitary person. She'd turned to Avery or Clara from time to time. But really, Nan had always been her person. Now Nan needed her to be the strong one.

The last person on earth she would have turned to for help was standing at her side. That took her by surprise.

"Thank you," she said. "For understanding and for letting me talk."

They entered Tilly's together, searching the café for Nan. She was sitting in the back, Tilly at her side. When she saw Emery, she smiled and waved, pretending, as she often did, that everything was as it should be.

Emery's heart ached knowing these first stages would lead to worsening symptoms. It might take years. Or months. There was no way of knowing.

Beau gave her hand a gentle squeeze.

"Tilly called you," Nan said when Emery walked up to her table. She gave her friend Tilly a frustrated look. "I told you I would be fine."

"I knew you'd be fine, too." Tilly put a hand on Nan's shoulder. "But I also know when to ask for help. You needed one of your girls."

Nan sighed. "I couldn't remember how to get home," she admitted. "Tilly and I had coconut cream pie, then we sat and talked a bit. I'm fine now."

"I know you are. It looks like you've had a good lunch," Emery teased, pointing to the remnants of the pie.

"It was the best. It always is." Nan sighed. "I guess you're here to take me home?"

"I am."

Nan looked from Emery to Beau. "Why is he standing over us like the warden?"

"He's helping," Emery confided, pretending he wasn't there to hear.

"Should I be worried?" Nan leaned close to ask.

"Not at all. He's being very nice."

"Don't you hurt my girl," Nan warned.

"Nan…" Emery said, hoping to stop a conversation that could get awkward.

"I wouldn't dream of it," Beau cut in, giving Emery a quick look of understanding.

"I see." Nan reached for her cup of coffee, but it was empty. "I do think you've become a better man."

Emery buried her face in her hands. "Nan, please."

"Well, it wouldn't hurt you to go on a date," Nan informed her. "I'm sure he'll be mighty handsome if he shaves and stops looking so sickly."

"I'm sure I'll be very handsome," Beau said with a cheeky grin.

"Very handsome and very charming. What happened to you, Beau Wilde? I don't remember you being quite so charming when you were a young man."

Beau leaned down to whisper in Nan's ear. Nan nodded at whatever he'd told her and then she patted his hand, as if the two had come to an understanding.

Emery didn't want to know his secrets. She didn't want to think about his looks, his random acts of kindness or how it had felt when he held her hand, ever so briefly.

"Unless the two of you are in a hurry, you should feed those girls," Nan said after teasing Emery.

Teasing Emery. He glanced her way, and when she made quick eye contact with him, he remembered a moment from the past, a moment that until now he'd managed to forget. A moment when those gray eyes had looked his way with hurt and humiliation that his words had caused, and he hadn't cared. She'd been sixteen, quiet and unusual. And he'd tried to destroy her.

Briefly he closed his eyes against the pain the memory caused and called himself a coward, because his guilt was nothing compared to the hurt he'd caused her.

He would make amends. Somehow, someway, if she'd let him.

"Finally," Charlie said, her words bringing him back to the present. "I want a cheeseburger and fries. Cadence wants chicken strips and tater tots."

"Why don't we let Cadence tell us what she wants," Beau said.

Charlie rolled her eyes. "Because she *can't*."

"I think Cadence would probably like to choose her own food," Emery inserted. She pushed a menu to the child and pointed to the children's selection. "Chicken strips, mac and cheese, hot dog, hamburger. What do you think?"

Her gentleness eased the tightness in his chest.

Cadence pointed.

"Mac and cheese." Emery dropped a kiss on

the child's head. "Do you want fries or tater tots?"

Cadence blinked and then pointed to the left-over fries on Nan's plate. She'd always been so full of joy, laughter and sunshine. Beau could still see that little girl was in there, but how could they reach her?

Conversation resumed as they waited for their food. Nan told a story about the boat she'd been working on, then hesitated, looking around the café, as if searching for someone.

"Nan, are you okay?" Emery asked.

Nan reached for her soda, her hand trembling a bit as she lifted it. "I'm good, Emmy. I just thought for a moment that I saw someone."

She took a sip, then laughed. "Silly me. It's just Chester. You'd think that man could eat at home at least one day a week."

"You would think," Emery agreed.

As if on cue, Chester Clark scooted his chair back and headed their way. When he reached them, he grabbed a chair from a neighboring table and pulled it over.

"Mind if I sit a spell?" he asked Nan.

"Well, it appears to me, Chester Clark, that you're already sitting."

He grinned at the rebuff. "Nan, stop pretending you don't like me."

"I never have, Chester."

"I came over to ask Beau if he's planning on taking up farming again." Chester dropped a quarter in front of Cadence as he waited for Beau's response. "I bet you like gumballs. Have that cheap feller right there take you to the machine before you all leave. It's one of them fancy kind that twirls down and shoots the gum out at the bottom."

Cadence glanced from the quarter to Beau and back to the quarter. He nodded and she slid the quarter off the table and held it tight in her hand.

"Put it in your pocket, Caddie." Charlie helped her sister, then whispered something to her. Charlie sighed. "She says thank you."

"That's okay, little bit. You're welcome." Chester ruffled her hair, then he turned his attention back to Beau, blinking to fend off tears in his eyes.

Beau liked the older farmer. Chester always seemed like a bit of a curmudgeon, but his heart was good. In addition to farming, he'd also worked part-time as a bus driver. The thing Beau remembered about Chester was that, as much as he might sound like he was growling, he had cared about the kids on his bus route. He'd bought Christmas presents for those who didn't have a lot and delivered food to those in need.

Chester repeated his question about farming, not letting Beau off the hook. "I'd definitely rather be farming," Beau responded. "But I'm afraid my dad might be enjoying retirement a bit too much, which leaves me to run the dealerships."

"Well, if you boys think you need a bit of land, Della Jones asked me to sell that thirty acres your brother is leasing plus another two hundred across the highway."

"I'll let Ethan know," Beau said. He almost said he'd like to buy that land. His own land, his own career, his own choices.

He loved his life in Tulsa, but having a career of his own choosing, instead of working for his father, and maybe a place where he'd like to grow old, those things were becoming more important to him.

Tilly arrived with their food.

"See you all later," Chester said as he left them to rejoin his table. They were a common sight at Tilly's, that group of farmers. They worked hard every day of the week, but in the afternoon a person would see their trucks lined up in front of the café. They'd go in for lunch, coffee and the latest local news. Otherwise known as gossip.

As they turned their attention to their lunches, Nan sneaked a few fries to Zeb.

"I saw that," Emery said after a half dozen fries had been swept off the plate.

"I'm not sure what you're talking about," Nan said with a smirk, then winked at Cadence.

The little girl, all strawberry blond curls and big blue eyes, grinned at Nan and dropped one of her fries on the floor.

"You're such a bad influence," Emery chastised without malice.

"It comes with age," Nan said as she reached for a napkin. "I can say what everyone else is thinking but too afraid to say."

After lunch was eaten, they left the diner. Nan walked ahead with Charlie and Cadence. Charlie kept up a steady stream of conversation. Cadence held tight to Zeb's harness. The dog kept a slow pace for the child and occasionally glanced up, as if making sure that the little girl was okay.

That left Emery at Beau's side. He thought he should say something, about the earlier memory that still haunted him, and about the absence of her smile and wondering if he'd been the one to steal it away. If so, could he bring it back?

"I assume you want to drive Nan's car and not my truck," he said as they neared the vehicles parked at the side of the café.

"You would be correct. The less often I have to climb in that truck, the happier I'll be." She grimaced after the words left her mouth. "Not that I can't..."

"It's okay. I understand."

"Let me start over. I appreciate your help today. I think having you and the girls at the table made it easier for her. And for me."

"It's me who owes you, because you and Nan have been here for the girls." The next part was the harder thing to say, to admit. "And I owe you for the way I treated you in the past."

She glanced away, her eyes straying to where Nan and the girls were getting in Nan's car. "I prefer not to think about those years."

"And I haven't thought about them enough," he admitted. "This apology is long overdue."

"It's in the past," she said, a little lighter, her eyes reflecting a woman who had moved on. "Thank you for apologizing. Now, let's focus on the present."

She held out her hand, offering a truce. He took it, holding her hand gently.

"I look forward to knowing you better, Emery. Maybe we can even be friends."

"Maybe," she said. The lingering doubt in her expression made him wonder if she meant it. She was kind. She hadn't denied him the chance to apologize, to ask forgiveness.

But an apology didn't mean a friendship.

"Looks as if the girls are riding with Nan and me," she said as she made to walk away.

"It looks that way."

The conversation ended on that note, with Emery leaving him standing in the parking lot of Tilly's, wishing he'd been a better person all of those years ago.

The man he was today, *that* man wanted a second chance. The thought made him falter as he headed toward his truck. The last thing he needed right now was to let his thoughts wander in that direction, in *her* direction.

He had one purpose for being in Pleasant. To be here for Cadence and Charlie. Anything else was pure selfishness on his part.

Including his attraction to Emery Guthrie.

Chapter Six

The bells of Pleasant Community Church pealed through the stillness of the country morning, announcing to all that church would begin in five minutes. As the bell rang, cars pulled into the gravel parking lot and parishioners continued to make their way inside.

Emery waited at the car as Nan found her Bible and the basket of cookies she would pass out to visitors. She waved to friends as they hurried up the sidewalk and felt a moment of happiness. Avery and her husband, Grayson, were a part of the last-minute crowd that hurried for the doors of the church. Their daughter Quinn went around them, in a rush to see friends. Baby Alexis patted at Grayson's cheeks.

Emery loved this church, not only because her family attended, but also because it had been a safe haven for her as a child.

Back then, her neighbor Franny Meyers had picked her up every Sunday morning for church, handing her a doughnut and carton of chocolate milk as soon as she'd gotten situated in the back seat of Franny's old Jeep.

She smiled thinking of those days and the Sunday school teacher.

"Here we go," Nan said as she gathered up her purse and her Bible in its embroidered case. Emery took the basket of cookies.

"Got it all?" Emery asked.

"I think so." Nan gave her a discerning look. "You're okay?"

"I'm good," she answered.

"Looks as if Beau made it to church with the girls."

Emery glanced in the direction Nan indicated. Beau had parked at the end of the parking lot, and he was herding the girls toward the church. They had made it on time, but none of them looked happy.

Cadence wore her ever-present sadness, a look that made a person's heart ache. Charlie frowned big enough to let everyone know to steer clear. Beau seemed pale. For a man who kept a summer tan almost all year, that was concerning. As they drew closer, Emery could see the tight lines at the corners of his mouth and the furrow between his brows.

Nan noticed also. "Beau Wilde, what is the matter with you?"

"He's sick. I told him we should stay home." Charlie rolled her eyes and kept walking. Emery thought she saw a flash of concern on the girl's face.

"I'm fine," Beau insisted, flashing dimples that charmed Nan but didn't fool Emery. "I just overslept."

"Where's your brother?" Nan asked.

"A cow got down and he's been up all night with her. The veterinarian is supposed to be showing up anytime."

"Emery," someone called from behind them.

"Is that Louis Stanford?" Nan asked.

"Yes, it is." Emery hesitated in walking away from Nan, but Louis looked worried, and he never let anything get to him. She also didn't want him to mention in front of Nan or Beau the job position he'd told her about the previous day.

"You go ahead and talk. Charlie and I will go on inside," Nan said. "Charlie, grab that basket from Emery."

"Where's Zeb?" Beau asked after Nan and Charlie made their way inside. Cadence remained but stayed close to Emery.

"Home having a well-deserved day off," Emery answered. She petted Cadence's hair and the child smiled up at her. She wanted to pick her up and hold her close.

"I'll wait for you," Beau said. That explained why he stood next to her as the juvenile officer came toward them.

"You don't have to," she told him. She really wished he wouldn't. "You look as if you need to go inside and sit down."

"I'm fine," Beau told her as he leaned to pick up Cadence. "I woke up with a headache. Residual effect of the virus."

"Emery, I'm sorry to bother you." Louis stepped in front of her, winded from the fast walk from the parking lot. He put his hand to his chest and took a deep breath. "I'm getting too old for this job."

"I'm sure you could still beat most of us in a footrace," she teased.

"I'm not so sure," he said, still taking deep breaths. "I won't keep you long. I only wanted to touch base about the garden. I have a few more teens that I'd like to have volunteer if you're willing to oversee their community service."

"Gladly," she told him without hesitating. She'd never been very good at saying no to children in need. "We will meet again next Saturday at ten."

"Perfect. I'll have the parents bring their children by. I'd bring them myself, but I want some parental responsibility. If I send you a text with names, could you let me know that they show up? And keep me updated on Alex. I want him there every Saturday."

"No problem. How long would you like for them to work?"

"Every chance they get for an hour or two at a time."

"Send me the list and I'll make sure it happens."

"Thank you." He gave a salute, fingers to his thinning hairline. "My wife went on in and I see you have people waiting, but don't forget our conversation. I don't want to push, but if you could give me an idea what direction you're thinking…"

"I'll let you know," she said, silently praying that he wouldn't say more. The juvenile officer left them to catch up with his wife. Beau didn't ask questions. She breathed a sigh of relief, because she didn't want to discuss the job offer. She didn't want to admit that she'd always dreamed of such a position. She loved her job at the school, but to have a position in a residential facility had always been her goal.

As they neared the church entrance, Beau paused. He drew in a breath and then briefly closed his eyes. Emery hesitated next to him, her hand reached out, resting on his arm.

"This seems more than a headache," she said.

With his free hand, he rubbed his temple. "I'm fine. It'll pass."

She studied him for a moment and he smiled, as if to prove his assurance that it would pass.

She cared. That had always been her problem. Injured animals—and humans—were her downfall. A black terrier on the side of the road had bitten her hand and she'd needed stitches and a rabies shot. Tamara Baker crying in the bathroom senior year. Emery had offered her a tissue and sat with her until she calmed down. The next day, Tamara had started rumors about Emery.

She had to move past that feeling of always thinking someone was about to jerk the rug out from under her. She couldn't let that fear stop her from being who God called her to be. She couldn't let fear stop her from showing compassion.

She really wanted to be able to trust people, to widen her small circle of friends and family whom she did trust. But this man? She was trying not to question God, but she kept wondering, why this man?

As if God heard her and wanted to prove a point, Beau followed her down the aisle of the church. When she sat, he slid in next to her, still holding Cadence. In a church full of people he'd known most of his life, many he considered friends, he'd decided to sit next to her.

She shot him a quick look.

"What?"

"Nan would say you're green around the gills," she told him.

She opened her arms to Cadence. The child moved onto her lap, her thumb immediately going to her mouth.

"Fish analogies, my favorite."

"It draws a picture," she said.

"I'm fine," he assured her.

Throughout the service she continued to watch him, even as she listened to Pastor Matthews's sermon on caring for others. It stung a little, because she didn't want to care for Beau Wilde. She wanted to put him back in the neat little box where he was a one-dimensional character from her past. He shouldn't have layers. He should be frozen in time the way she remembered him.

Unfortunately, when the sermon ended, he stood when she did and prepared to leave the church as she left. He reached for Cadence's hand when she moved to his side.

Charlie joined them as they exited the building, avoiding the groups of people that congregated to talk about everything from the sermon to the lack of rain and where they planned to go for lunch.

The teenager took Cadence from Beau. "What's wrong with you?"

She sounded flippant, but there was an edge to her voice and a softness about her eyes. She was worried.

"He needs to rest," Emery told her.

"He looks sick to me," Charlie continued. "Obviously the handful of medicine he took this morning isn't helping."

"Handful?" Emery shot him a look and he shook his head.

"She's exaggerating," he told her as he pulled his keys out of his pocket.

"I think you should let me drive you home." The words were out and she couldn't drag them back.

"Are you sure?" he asked.

Was she sure? Of course she wasn't sure. She didn't want to get hurt and Beau Wilde could—probably would in some way—hurt her. But he was undeniably handsome. He was kind to children. He'd stayed at her side when she needed him the previous day.

God had a plan. And it looked as if His plan was to put Beau Wilde in her life.

* * *

The offer she'd made, to drive him, left her looking unsure. He sympathized, he really did, but at the moment, the headache took precedence.

"What about Nan?" he asked, blinking against the sunlight and wishing he had his sunglasses. If he could just get to his truck, he'd be fine.

"We brought her car and she's going to lunch with Avery and Grayson." Emery remained at his side.

"Were you supposed to go to lunch with your family?"

"No worries, I enjoy getting out of social engagements. I'm something like a hermit. I just need to let them know what's going on."

He started to object. But he couldn't, though. He had Charlie and Cadence to think about. The two stood near the truck, matching looks of concern on their faces.

"We'll wait for you," he said, caving. Pushing the unlock button on the remote, he opened the back door for the girls.

After making sure Charlie got Cadence buckled in, he walked around the truck. His attention strayed to Emery. He realized that when she was away from him, she became animated. Beautiful. Still serious, but even from a distance, he could see the light expression on her face. She intrigued him, this woman who rarely smiled, but whose eyes were often soft with compassion, with caring. He found himself wanting to hold her hand, because in brief moments when their hands had touched, he'd realized her skin was soft and he liked the way her fingers wrapped around his and squeezed before letting go. He liked that her hair smelled of something light and herbal and that she didn't use makeup to accentuate the smoky gray eyes that he couldn't help but get lost in.

All of those warm thoughts evaporated when Charlie leaned over the seat to study his face.

"Are you having a stroke or something?" the teen asked.

"I'm fine," he assured her. "The medicine I took for the headache is starting to kick in." Which meant it no longer felt like a stabbing pain through his skull.

"I don't know, you still look kinda green," she informed him.

"You are trouble," Beau told the teen.

"Maybe," she agreed. "But I'm guessing the way you look at Emery is trouble, too."

Before he could respond, Emery returned to the truck. Through the windshield, she made quick eye contact with him. Her troubled expression had to do with him, with his truck and probably her desire to find a way out of the offer she'd made. Even her troubled expressions were intriguing.

"Ready to go?" Emery asked as she opened the driver's side door of his truck. She folded the crutch, shoved it in next to him, then grabbed the steering wheel to pull herself up.

"I'm hungry," Charlie spoke up as Emery started the truck. "And Cadence is crying."

"Why is Cadence crying?" Beau asked as he glanced in the back seat.

"She's probably hungry," Charlie answered with an eye roll.

Time to step up to the parenting plate. "Charlie, I appreciate that you think I'm clueless, but there is one thing I know without a doubt." He let her give him a questioning look and then he finished. "I don't need that look from you every time I say something. You can stop on your own or I'll find a consequence that encourages you to stop."

Emery made a sound of surprise. Charlie's eyes widened.

"Okay," she said. It was as if she'd been waiting for the moment when he stepped into the role of parent.

"Thank you. And we will get food." He winked at Cadence. "Chicken strips."

The little girl nodded and her tears disappeared.

That was when he noticed Emery studying the gearshift with more interest than seemed necessary. "What are you doing?" he asked.

"Figuring this out." She grimaced as she pushed the clutch and shifted into Reverse. She turned the ignition before he could stop her. The truck started, shuddered, died.

"You have to keep your foot on the clutch," he explained. "Clutch and brake, but then ease up on both."

"Got it." She bit down on her bottom lip as she concentrated on the process.

It was shaky, but she managed to get the truck out of the parking space.

"Now shift to First," he said.

She did, but without the clutch. Again, the truck died.

"I should have thought about you not knowing how to drive a standard."

"Yes, we should have, shouldn't we?" At that point, it would have been safer, easier, less painful for him to take over. Unfortunately, he was having too much fun watching her.

Before, she'd been beautiful. This brought out the cute and he liked her a lot this way.

"It's not as easy as I thought it would be." She eased forward again and the truck stuttered and died.

Charlie laughed and even Cadence giggled.

"This isn't going to work," Beau said as she started the truck again and eased on the gas while letting off the clutch too quickly. The truck bucked a bit, but it kept moving.

"I'm determined." She gave him a quick look but then returned her attention to the road and driving.

"You have to be more than determined," he said, leaning back in the seat. "Slow and steady."

They had an audience. Church members who hadn't made it to their cars were stopping to watch. One older man in overalls started their way, as if he meant to help. Beau stopped him with a wave of his hand. If she was determined to try, he would give her every opportunity to do her best.

"Okay, foot on the clutch, first gear, gas and ease off the clutch."

"Got it," she said. "No sudden moves."

"That's one way of putting it. As soon as you get on the road, you're going to speed up and shift to Second. You'll hear the engine whine as the RPM go up. That's your cue to shift again."

She laughed a little and glanced his way, her eyes bright with the adventure of driving his truck while he did his best to hold on and fight the headache that had dulled but now made him nauseated. Or maybe it was the ride.

A while later, they were on the road. The truck shuddered, either from her bad driving or fear. He sympathized with the vehicle.

From the back seat, he heard "uh-oh."

It was a tiny thing, just two syllables, but Charlie shrieked and the truck juddered to a stop, the engine dying in the process. The car behind them slammed on their brakes and honked, mere feet from rear-ending Beau's truck.

"You can't do that," Beau said as he waved to the folks behind them. He was rethinking the idea that this had been fun, or that it had been a wise decision on his part.

"I know. I know. But..." Emery took a deep breath and he could see tears shimmering at the surface of her eyes but not falling. He got it. Cadence had spoken for the first time since her parents' death.

She drew in another breath and managed a cheerful facade. "No big deal. I can drive this truck."

He turned, smiling at the little girl who had just shocked them all, maybe even herself. And Charlie, who seemed to be doing her best to hold it together. It was a wonder they weren't all crying, except Cadence, who seemed to be oblivious to the fact that she'd just spoken her first word in a month.

Two syllables, but it meant everything. It changed everything.

"We're holding up traffic," Charlie reminded with a wobble in her voice.

"Right, traffic." Emery started the truck and he cringed at the way she held the key too long. She made it to second gear, though. That was something.

The truck drove smoothly at a speed that wouldn't get them anywhere very fast. Tears trickled down Emery's face as her hand held the gearshift. Beau moved his hand to cover hers.

"I did it," she said.

"Did what?" he asked, confused.

"Drove a standard truck," she answered with a twinkle in her gray eyes. "And now I'm done. I don't think my leg is strong enough to keep up the constant shifting. I also don't think your nerves can take it much longer."

"I wasn't going to say anything," he told her with a wink. "But I have to agree. I think we're all ready to end this driving lesson."

She laughed a little, sounding younger and more carefree. She should laugh more often. And smile. He realized it was a rare gem, her smile. She hit the turn signal and pulled into the empty parking lot of the Farm and Home store.

The truck jerked to a stop as she shifted into First and hit the brake.

"Thank You, God!" Charlie said. "And before anyone gets on me, I mean that. I've been seriously praying back here. And you all heard Cadence. You're lucky she didn't say some bad words."

In that moment, it didn't matter how it had happened. It just mattered that they were all together and life felt right. Cadence had spoken, Charlie was acting more like the girl he'd always known and he was sitting next to a woman who made him want this to be his every day.

Until that moment, he hadn't realized what he'd been feeling the past couple of years was an emptiness meant to be filled by someone.

This, he told God in a silent prayer. *This is what I want.*

"Are you sure you feel well enough to drive?" Emery asked.

The question startled him back to the present.

"I think I have to," he teased. "But you did great."

"No need to lie. I know it was terrible."

He told her how to set the emergency brake and then the two of them got out and circled to switch sides. They met at the back of the truck. When she stopped in front of him, it threw him a little off balance. He couldn't tell if it was remnants of the headache, the harrowing five minutes of her driving or just her. She unsettled him.

He'd never been unsettled.

No, that wasn't true. The night he went to church in Tulsa, when he was twenty-two and thought he owned the world. He'd come to the realization that night that he wasn't so good, nor as important as he'd thought. He'd realized that he'd spent a lot of years going to church, living his parents' faith and not having much of his own. It had shaken him, knowing he needed to find his own faith because he couldn't go to God on the shirttails of his father.

That had been a moment. This moment came on a different level.

So there she stood in front of him, her dark hair pulled back in a messy bun, her gray eyes troubled. She was worried about him. She didn't want to be, he knew that. He was the last person she wanted to think about, care about or even like.

He didn't blame her. Yet he wanted her to care about him. The level of need he felt for her friendship was astounding.

"Are you sure you can drive?" she asked, her voice hesitant as she looked him over.

"I'm sure." He couldn't help but tease, "Better than you."

"I tried," she informed him. Her lips lifted up

at the corners and her eyes sparkled with hidden mischief.

He wanted to make her smile. More than that, he wanted to discover the woman hiding beneath the serious demeanor. The sparkle in her eyes told him she had layers that maybe she had yet to discover.

"Cadence spoke. That made it all worth it."

The hint of a smile became the real thing, like a butterfly emerging from a cocoon. "Yes, she did."

"You rarely smile," he noted. The words were out before he could stop them.

Her eyes widened and the smile dissolved. "Why would you say that?"

"I'm sorry. It's just something I've noticed."

"I smile," she said.

"Yes, but not often enough."

"I save it for moments that matter."

"Then I think you should have more of those moments." He might have to create them himself. He wondered what it would take. Flowers? A kitten?

Her lips parted. He'd shocked her. She would have been even more shocked if she'd known he wanted to kiss her.

"Hey, we need to eat lunch." Charlie's head was out the back window.

"Lunch," he said to Emery.

"Yes," she agreed, without seeming to realize what she'd agreed to.

They parted. He went to the driver's side, she to the passenger side. The trip home was smoother and less stressful, but not nearly as fun. In the silence of the cab, he found himself thinking about the woman he'd been dating back in Tulsa, Sarah. He hadn't talked to her since the day he'd landed in Kansas City. It had been a brief conversation to tell her he was home from his mission trip. He hadn't told her about his illness. He hadn't told her about his guardianship of Cadence and Charlie.

There had been a time when he'd thought she might be important to him. But Emery had him rethinking everything. The only problem was, she didn't seem to want to like him.

Chapter Seven

On Thursday, Emery was beginning to question if this school year would ever end. She'd spent the past hour talking to two girls about a rumor they'd spread, destroying someone's reputation out of spite. Earlier in the week she'd been forced to call Protective Services for suspected abuse of a first grader. She really disliked making those calls, but it was required by law, and she wouldn't know how to live with herself if something happened to a child.

As she left the teachers' lounge with a soda and some chocolate, her phone buzzed. At her side, Zeb glanced up. Either he wanted a bite of the candy or he was annoyed by the buzzing of her phone for the tenth time in an hour.

She glanced at her phone. Another text from Louis Stanford. The residential facility was desperate to discuss the job opportunity with her.

Apparently, they were willing to make it worth her while with a salary and benefit package that was astounding. She shook her head, not wanting to think about the temptation. But her willpower was fading, because they were closing in on the end of what had been a very long and trying school year.

Six more days.

Six more days and it would be time to say goodbye to Beau and the girls. With so much to accomplish, she should surely be able to keep her mind from wandering to Beau Wilde, but wander it did. Since Sunday, she'd spent too much time thinking about him. Wondering how he was doing with the girls. How they would manage once they got to Tulsa. She'd thought about them, but when she'd seen them at church on Wednesday, true to her nature, she'd avoided them. That seemed safest.

It protected her heart, a heart that found it easy to overlook the past and too easy to care. Caring wasn't a fault, she'd often told herself. Caring was what Nan did. But there was a safe way to care and a dangerous way. She always rushed headlong into the dangerous path, the path that led her to trust and then regret when the person hurt her.

Her own mother topped the list of people who had hurt her.

Brushing off those thoughts, she walked through the door of her office and into what smelled like a flower garden gone wild. A vase sat in the center of her desk, an enormous, over-the-top arrangement of lilies, daisies and roses in bright yellows, oranges and pinks with white freesia interspersed.

"Oh my," she said to no one. Zeb looked up at her, his head cocked to the side. "It's a ridiculous amount of flowers," she explained to the dog. "I don't think I've ever received flowers from anyone."

"Is it your birthday?"

She swept a glance from the flowers to the woman standing in the doorway. Paula Winters, the kindergarten teacher. Zeb hadn't been the only one listening.

"No, it isn't."

"Are you keeping secrets?" Paula teased. "Because you're right, that is a ridiculous amount of flowers. Definitely not from a parent. Unless the parent has a huge crush on you."

"I promise you I have no crushes and no one has a crush on me." She leaned heavily on her crutch and studied the flowers.

"Stop acting like someone put a bomb on your desk. Read the card." Paula stepped past her and slipped the card from the plastic holder. "It's that simple, my friend. Also, you need to embrace that you are a beautiful, accomplished, kind woman, and any man would love to date you. If only you didn't scare them off with that serious frown of yours."

"I'm not scary. And…" She took the card out of the envelope, smiling at her friend as she did. "See. I did it."

A different kind of smile pulled at her lips, the kind of smile she felt growing from the inside.

"Whoa, I don't think I've seen that before. I've seen your professional smile. I've seen your 'kids' smile. But that smile is one I haven't witnessed."

"Stop," Emery said, heat lapping at her cheeks.

"What does that card say?"

"It's silly," she said. "And I'm not reading it to you because it's private."

Paula glanced at her watch. "I have to pick my kiddos up from PE, so you're getting a break this time. But a woman without a crush does not smile like that."

"It isn't a crush," she called out to her friend's retreating back. "I don't even like him. He…"

She'd said too much. At the door, Paula paused and looked back.

"He?" Paula winked. "That means a crush."

"I'm not twelve," she informed her friend, in

a voice that was petulant and definitely made her sound twelve.

"No, you're almost thirty and you need to date a nice guy."

"You should go."

Of course, she didn't.

Emery read the card a second time, keeping it away from Paula's curious eyes. *Caught you smiling. You should do it more often. Beau.*

Paula's head tilted to the side, much the same way that Zeb's did.

"Interesting. We'll talk later, when we work on that garden of yours."

"We won't talk," Emery said firmly. "But I do appreciate your help with the garden."

Paula started to leave. Emery stopped her.

"How is Cadence doing?"

Paula glanced down the hall and then stepped back in the room.

"She's a little better. She's playing with the other children. She smiles more. Mrs. Graves had her for almost an hour yesterday and she came back with a stuffed animal. I'm hoping that meant a successful session."

Mrs. Graves worked within the school system two half days a week. It was a tremendous help, having a therapist in the building for students who needed her services.

"Sunday she said, 'uh-oh.' I know that isn't a lot, but it seemed huge."

"Why uh-oh?" Paula asked.

"It might have been my driving. I had to take them home and I was driving…" Caught.

Paula's eyes widened and then she burst out laughing. "Uh-oh."

"What?" Emery asked, glancing at the card in her hand and forcing herself to remain straight-faced even as heat spread across her cheeks.

"I'm very good at basic math," Paula said with another burst of laughter. "Two plus two. Now I know who the flowers are from and who is putting that rare smile on your face."

"Go away now," Emery said as she shooed her friend toward the door. "You have children waiting for you and Coach Gates doesn't like it when teachers are late picking students up from PE."

She didn't have a crush, Emery assured herself as she peeked at the card again and then leaned to sniff the fragrant roses in the bouquet. She knew better than to have any kind of feelings for Beau Wilde.

Years ago she'd made that mistake, charmed by his smile and a single moment of kindness. The next day he'd told everyone that the 'crippled girl' had a crush on him. He'd laughed and tormented her, asking if she really thought he'd invite her to the school dance. How would she ever be able to dance when she could barely walk?

Her heart ached at the memory. She'd been recovering from another surgery on her leg at the time.

The surgery had been deemed a success by the doctors. She sometimes needed two crutches, on the days when the pain or inflammation were at their worst, but most days she managed with one and she lived her best life, in spite of what her father had done to her.

He'd caught her trying to leave the house. She'd packed a bag and waited until he passed out, him and his friends. Unfortunately, one of them roused and saw her slipping out the back door. When he'd caught her, her father had told her she would never run from him again. Ever.

Then he'd locked her away in the basement, thinking no one would know what he'd done to her.

The memories started to suffocate her. She blinked them away and sat down at her desk, pulling Zeb close and praying for peace. God had given her a second chance, a new family and hope. She wasn't going to waste what He had done for her by dwelling on the past.

Her phone buzzed. She glanced at the text,

grabbed her crutch, fixing it to her left forearm, then she reached for Zeb's leash.

"Work to do, Zeb." At her words, the dog clambered to his feet and gave her a steady look.

Thirty seconds. That was all it took to turn the corner of the hall and see the problem. Thirteen-year-old Alex stood in the center of the hallway, a staff member standing nearby, trying to coax him into doing what she asked.

"I said I'm not going to art," the boy said, holding a basketball under his arm as he made his most menacing face. He stepped closer to the aide, a woman just over five feet tall. "I'm not going to draw stupid pictures of flowers."

"I'm sorry you don't want to go," Mrs. Pointer told him. "Could you tell me why? And if you think there is an alternative, what would it be?"

"I'm going home," he said as he pushed past her. "I'm sick of you all telling me what to do every hour of the day."

Emery moved to the center of the hall as he came toward her.

"Hey, Alex," she said with her most cheerful tone. "How's it going?"

"Great, now they're sending you to try and make me do what they want."

She shrugged. "Who is *they*?"

"This whole stupid school," he growled. "People are always in my business, telling me what to do."

"Oh, I see. That's tough. It happens to me, too. They tell me what time to be here, how late to stay, when to take lunch."

"Don't give me one of your lectures about life and rules." He started past her and she decided her best bet was to walk with him. "You and your stupid garden."

"Yeah, life and rules. It stinks. I'm guessing there is more going on with you than a dislike of painting flowers."

"No, there isn't. You always think there's more going on than there is. My dad said it was probably you that called the state on us. And if it was, thanks a lot, because I got blamed."

"I'm sorry that your dad was angry with you." She hadn't made the call.

"Whatever," he said. "I'm leaving."

"I can't let you do that." She searched the hall for the vice principal, who should have been called to help in this situation. If Alex went out the door, she wouldn't be able to stop him. He was a half foot taller than her and she definitely couldn't run him down. He was bigger, heavier and faster.

"You can't stop me," Alex said. His blond hair fell down in his face, giving him a boyish look.

He was a boy, but the size of a grown man and with a temper to match.

He lowered his voice and gave her a pleading look. "Please let me go."

"I can't."

She believed that given a different set of circumstances, Alex, like so many children, would have been a different person with a different future. He just needed someone to show him that he mattered.

As he headed for the door, she tried to move in front of him to talk to him. The push against her shoulders took her by surprise. Her back hit the wall and he peered down at her with all of that anger pouring from his eyes, his expression.

"I said, do *not* try to stop me." He towered over her, and when she started to move, he shoved again.

Zeb barked and tried to get between them. He growled a warning to the boy.

"I'll kill that dog," Alex said.

"Zeb, sit." Her voice shook as she gave the command. Zeb didn't sit, but he moved closer to her side. She straightened, took a chance and moved a few inches from the wall. The last thing she wanted was to look weak or vulnerable. "Alex, don't touch me again."

"Who will stop me?" he asked.

She gave him a hard stare. "If I have to, I will. I've met more than one bully in my life. I had hoped you weren't one, but if you're going to shove me again, I want you to know I won't let it happen."

"I'm going out that door."

"No, you're not." The voice, masculine, authoritative and familiar, came from the left, just out of Emery's line of sight.

A moment later he stood between them. Beau gave her a quick, assessing look and then focused on the teen. Alex was large for his age. But Beau was taller, broader across the shoulders and unafraid.

"Who are you?" Alex asked.

"A friend."

"Of hers?" The boy shot her a look and then he laughed. "You have a boyfriend?"

"Just a friend," Beau spoke firmly. "I can be your friend, too, if you need one. But I'm going to have to ask you to step away from the lady."

As much as she didn't want to admit it, she was thankful for Beau's interference. He'd arrived just in time.

Mr. Holden, the school vice principal, came around the corner of the hall. With him was the high school principal, Mr. Vance. Emery mumbled that it was about time. Her legs began to tremble, the aftereffects of adrenaline. She leaned back against the wall, needing the support.

"Alex, let's take a walk." Mr. Holden reached for the student, his hand going to the boy's arm.

Alex jerked away. "I can walk by myself."

"Fine, walk by yourself. But stay by my side."

"Fine."

Emery waited until they left and then she took a deep breath. "I need to go."

She whispered the words, or thought she did, and then she walked away. In twenty very long steps, she reached her office. Zeb stayed close to her. Beau followed her inside.

He pushed the door closed.

The moment the door closed, the office shrank and became a dark, dank basement. She should have opened the blinds before she left. She hated to have them closed. She needed sunlight. She needed the door open.

She reached for the handle, fighting wave after wave of panic that tore at her chest, at her lungs. She must have made a noise, because Zeb barked sharply and moved close.

Strong arms closed around her. She fought against him, her fists against his chest as she tried to get away, and then his voice reached past the haze of panic.

"You're safe now."

He wasn't her father. This wasn't the basement. She was safe and Beau Wilde held her close, as if she mattered.

As if he meant to keep her safe from all harm.

"Shhh," Beau whispered close to her ear as she fought, trying to free herself.

"The door. Please open the door." Her words came out harsh as she tried to breathe.

He did as she asked, partially opening the door, and then he did the only thing he knew to do. He scooped her up in his arms and carried her to the chair behind her desk.

He sat, still holding her close. It took several long minutes of him telling her she was safe, encouraging her to take slow even breaths before she began to relax in his arms.

He kissed her forehead. "You're safe," he told her again.

"I know," she whispered. Then she tensed, struggling against him. "I have to get up."

"Slowly," he warned.

She nodded but moved quickly, her hand leveraging the desk to steady herself. Beau gained his feet and hurried to grab the crutch she'd dropped to the floor as he lifted her. He handed it to her and then gave her a moment to find herself again.

"You were pretty amazing out there. You handled yourself well."

"Did I?" she asked, still feeling weak.

"You did," he assured her. Until she'd been overpowered. He wished he'd spoken up sooner, letting the teen know they weren't alone.

"Maybe, until that last little bit where I had a nervous breakdown in my office and you had to carry me to a seat." She avoided looking at him. "Thank you for that."

"Are you okay?"

She had moved to the windows and opened them to let in some fresh air.

"I'm a little claustrophobic," she said to the open window.

A little, he thought, might have been an understatement.

"I usually have the door open and the blinds up. I don't particularly care for the dark or being enclosed," she said, looking back over her shoulder. "When Alex towered over me like that, it brought back some memories I'd rather not relive anytime soon."

"I'm sorry," he said. The words seemed pathetically inadequate.

Her attention moved to the flowers on her desk and he saw the corner of her mouth twitch. "Thank you for the flowers...and the smile."

"I'd do it every day if it wouldn't get me in trouble."

"I'm sure it would cause people to talk."

They stood in silence for a moment and he gave her that time. She seemed to need it, to gather herself and regain her composure. Zeb understood, too. The dog remained close, a watchful eye on her face, as if sensing what her expressions meant.

"What are you doing here?" she asked. "I mean, other than to see if the flowers did their job. Also, why is my smile so important to you?"

"You're very direct." He didn't have an answer for the question about her smile, except that when she did, it changed everything.

"Yes, I am," she agreed. "I've found it makes life easier if I cut to the chase."

"I had to talk to the high school principal. Charlie got in trouble today. She punched a boy because he made fun of Cadence. They recommended she participate in the community garden. The principal thinks this idea of yours will teach the students to work together, but also show them self-reliance and doing for others."

"I hope that's what happens." She took a seat and studied him, her features now prim. He squirmed like a schoolboy caught tying braids in a knot. "I wish there was more we could do for Cadence and Charlie. Paula—Mrs. Winters—said she thought Cadence had a good meeting with Mrs. Graves. There's been more smiling lately."

"That's good to know." He rubbed a hand over his face. "But I'm still not sure I'm qualified for this parenting business."

"Who is? You are guaranteed to mess up, to make mistakes, but also you will love those girls and you'll learn. That's parenting."

He studied her upturned face, caught momentarily in a ray of sunshine that made her gray eyes silver and caught hints of auburn in her dark brown hair. As a teen, he'd seen nothing but what he perceived as her weakness.

He didn't deserve her kindness. Or her approval.

"Why are you looking at me like that?" she asked.

"I'm so sorry, Emery. For hurting you, for causing you pain."

"Is that why you sent the flowers?" Her voice grew soft and he saw the immediate pain in her eyes, even as she turned away from him.

"No, the flowers were because I wanted to make you smile, just like I wrote on the card."

"The flowers are beautiful," she told him. "They did make me smile. And thank you, for… everything. I hate falling apart."

"I'm glad I was here."

She hesitated. "I'm glad you were here, too."

He needed to lighten the mood, before this darkness swallowed them both. "So, the flowers did the trick?"

Her lips tugged upward, almost as if against her will. "Yes, they did the trick."

The admission pleased him.

It had become important to him in a way he hadn't quite figured out. If he could, he would make her smile every day. Or every hour, if she'd let him.

Not because he owed her, not to make amends, but because her smile opened up something inside of him.

She felt like the missing piece to his life. The thought shook him, because until now, he hadn't realized that anything had been missing.

Chapter Eight

Saturday morning, Nan and Emery rushed from the house. They were running late. They'd gotten sidetracked by housework, and then by a newborn calf that one of Nan's cows had delivered that morning. When Nan had called Emery out to the field, the mother Angus had been giving the tiny heifer calf her first meal. The calf had wobbled a bit as she searched for her breakfast, but once she caught on, she'd quickly become an expert.

Emery loved farm life. She'd lived in Springfield for several years, working as a caseworker for the Division of Family Services. She'd enjoyed her apartment, her job and city life, but coming home had reminded her how much she loved this farm and her small town.

If she accepted the offer Louis had put before her and continued to ask about, it would be back to city life, but on a whole new track. At the end of the year, she would have a doctorate. In her quest for more schooling, she might have studied herself out of a job, because she'd be overqualified for anything other than administration and she didn't want that. She wanted to continue working one-on-one with students.

As they hurried to the car, her phone rang. She glanced at the caller ID. "It's Beau," she told Nan.

"Better answer," Nan said. "Might be important."

She answered and heard Beau say "Have you left for the garden yet?" without preamble.

"We're just leaving now. We're running late."

He remained silent for a few seconds. Then said, "I'm going to make you even more late, but I'll make it up to you. I'll pull weeds. I'll be the water boy. I'll make you dinner."

"What's wrong?" she asked.

"Did you smile?" he asked, making her wish she hadn't put the call on speaker so Nan wouldn't have heard that.

"If this is such an emergency, why are you so concerned with my smile?"

"Interesting," Nan whispered to Zeb as he trotted next to her.

"We're having a hairbrush emergency," he admitted.

"That's a new one," Emery said. "We'll be there in five minutes."

"I owe you."

"Big-time," she told him.

Nan held out her car keys to Emery.

"I'd rather you drive," Nan said, by way of explanation.

"Are you sure?" Emery asked, keeping her tone light. "You know that my driving scares you."

"There comes a time in life when you have to pick the lesser of two evils," Nan said with a faint lift of her mouth, a failed attempt at humor. Emery couldn't laugh. "I've decided that your driving is less frightening than us getting lost. No one wants to end up on the wrong side of Pleasant."

"You're right, that side of town can be frightening. Even in broad daylight." They both knew that Pleasant didn't have a wrong side of town. "Nan…"

Nan held up her hand to stop her. "We're grown-ups and we both know what is going to happen. It might happen in six months or six years, but we know it's coming and I'm asking you to keep smiling. We will laugh. We will pray and we will find joy, even in this."

That was asking a lot. But for Nan, Emery

took a deep breath and smiled. "We are more than conquerors."

Nan quickly hugged her, let go and turned away. But not before Emery caught the shimmer of unshed tears in her eyes. She took that moment to brush away her own tears. Minutes later they were heading down the highway toward the Rocking W Ranch.

"This is a beautiful place," Nan said as they pulled up to the ranch house. "Too bad those boys are single and not filling it with grandchildren for Cora and Ben."

"Yes, it's a shame." Emery hurried from the car before Nan could make stronger hints.

The door opened before they were up the steps of the front porch. Charlie's eyes glimmered with amusement as she beckoned them inside.

"I told you he couldn't do this," Charlie said. "He can't even brush Cadence's hair."

They could hear Ethan and Beau inside. Emery and Nan found the men in the kitchen. Cadence was on the counter, silent, tearless and her eyes scrunched closed.

A hairbrush was wrapped up in her strawberry blond hair.

Beau glanced up, grimaced and went back to work trying to unsnarl the tangled curls from the brush. "I think we might have to cut it."

Cadence shook her head violently and tears streamed freely down her cheeks.

"We won't cut your hair, honey," Nan assured the little girl as she took over. "Goodness gracious, you've made a mess of this child's hair." She looked at Beau and blinked. "I reckon honesty is the best policy, but for the life of me, I can't think of your name."

"Beau," he answered. "I'm glad you're here to rescue us."

"Rescue you," Nan chuckled. "It seems we're here to rescue—" she smiled "—Caddie."

Cadence nodded, and then she cried, "Emmy."

Nan stepped back, stunned, and Emery grabbed the little girl up and held her close. "I've got you. I'm here."

Cadence leaned her head against her and held on, tears running down her cheeks. Emery closed her eyes, knowing that if she looked around the room, there wouldn't be a dry eye to be found. To prove the point, she saw Ethan quickly leave the kitchen.

She gave the child a last tight hug and sat her back on the counter.

"We're going to get you untangled and then Beau is going to take you to Tilly's for the biggest ice cream sundae she has." Emery kissed Cadence's cheek and got a watery smile. "We'll let Charlie go, too, if she can behave herself."

"We're going to need some conditioner," Nan informed Beau.

"Conditioner," he repeated.

Charlie rolled her eyes. "I'll get mine."

She was gone just a minute and returned with a bottle of conditioner. She handed it to Nan, who poured some in her hand, added a little water and worked it through the hair wrapped around the brush.

"Next time you comb or brush this child's hair, start at the bottom. Get the tangles out and things will go much better for you."

"I told them to braid her hair at night. Mo…" Charlie stopped herself with a stricken look on her face. She closed her eyes and shook her head.

"Charlie," Emery said, softly, hoping the girl would share. "It's okay to talk about them."

"It isn't okay. It won't bring them back." Charlie's expression morphed from sad to angry.

"No, it won't. But you should cherish those memories, all the things you did together, the things they did for you."

"It hurts too much," Charlie told them, a raw look of pain in her young eyes.

"I know it does." Emery took a step closer. "But maybe talking about them will make it hurt less."

Charlie shook her head, then, wonders of

wonders, she rushed to Beau and flung herself at him. Beau wrapped her in a hug.

"Maybe we can share memories," Beau said. "I have a lot, too."

She nodded against his shoulder. "Someday."

"Someday," Beau repeated. "When you're ready."

"When I don't hate myself so much," Charlie whispered.

"Why would you hate yourself?" Beau asked.

Emery glanced at Nan. Her foster mother kept working on Cadence's hair, but she shook her head, obviously not having the answer.

A look of fear spread across Cadence's face.

"Maybe we should sit outside?" Emery suggested. "Charlie?"

"I don't want to talk about it. Let's get Cadence's hair untangled and go. She deserves ice cream. She deserves it every single day."

Charlie pulled free from Beau's arms and stepped back, returning her mask of not caring back in place.

"This tangle is definitely stubborn," Nan said, as if nothing had happened.

Emery took the cue and moved to Nan's side. Nan handed over the brush. The curls were definitely a tangled mess. It seemed as if half the hair was wrapped from one direction, half the other direction. Emery looked at Beau, who now stood next to her.

"How in the world did you manage this?"

He shrugged and gave her a sheepish look. "Mad hair skills?"

Cadence giggled.

"Next time he picks up a brush, you should probably run," Emery advised the child as she continued to pull strands of hair from the brush.

"She should probably get two sundaes," Beau offered.

"And a pony," Charlie inserted.

Cadence nodded.

"A pretty golden pony," Charlie added, her voice back to normal but the emotional torment lingering in her eyes.

Emery continued to work on the tangled hair. Concentrating became more difficult as Beau leaned in close. She could feel the brush of his arm against hers and smell the spicy notes of his cologne.

"Almost done," she told Cadence. Thankfully.

She finally pulled the brush free. Cadence blinked, looking from Emery to the brush. The child looked so sweet, even with her tangled red-blond curls framing her face.

"Yeah! We did it!" Emery dropped a kiss on the top of Cadence's head. "You're free. Well, nearly free. I'm afraid we still need to brush your hair."

Cadence shook her head.

"Sorry, kiddo, it has to be done or it will just be more tangled later on." Emery started with a small strip of hair, working from the bottom up.

Beau remained at her side, watching. They had a lot they needed to discuss, she and Beau. About Charlie hating herself. And about Beau and his crusade to convince Emery that he was a better person than he'd been in high school.

She didn't need for him to prove himself to her.

"We should go," Nan reminded everyone.

"We're almost finished," Emery told her foster mom. "This wasn't so bad, was it, Caddie?"

Cadence wrinkled her nose.

"Right." Emery finished the last section of hair. "And we're done. Time for me to get out of here. I wouldn't want the kids to show up at the garden and me not be there."

"I'll walk out with you," Beau said. "Charlie, can you help Cadence get her shoes on?"

"So you can talk about me? I don't think so. Listen, the two of you can just forget what I said. I didn't mean it."

"It's okay, Charlie. We all say things we don't really mean." Emery gave Beau a look. "I can walk myself out to the car. We'll see you all at the church."

She grabbed the crutch she'd leaned against the counter, snapped her fingers for Zeb to follow and left. Without looking back, she knew that Nan would hug the girls, give Beau a sympathetic glance and then follow Emery out the door.

She prayed Nan wouldn't ask what was wrong with her, because Emery didn't have a clear answer, for her mother or for herself. She only knew that everything was twisted up and confusing right now.

She didn't want Beau to think he had to watch over her or keep her safe. Or think that he owed her smiles.

But the kinder he was, the more she wanted his genuine friendship and not his attempts at proving himself to her.

As Beau pulled up to the community church, he realized the days of always being early were gone. He glanced at the clock. Ten minutes late.

"You look like you just swallowed a bug," Charlie said from the back seat of the truck.

"We're late," he told her.

"So?"

So? "It's important to be places on time."

She actually laughed at him. "This isn't easy for you, is it?"

"No, it isn't, but we'll be okay."

She unbuckled Cadence and helped her out of the truck. "What would you be doing if you weren't stuck here with us?"

The question took him by surprise. For a moment Charlie looked and sounded far older than her fourteen years. She also looked unsure.

There were several answers to the question. Only one was right.

"I don't think I'd call myself 'stuck,'" he told her. She walked next to him, holding Cadence's hand. "I'm here because this is where I need to be. With you and Cadence."

"What would you call it, then? I mean, if it wasn't for us, you'd be in Tulsa, probably dating that pretty blonde you'd told my dad about. He thought you'd probably end up marrying her. Wasn't she a beauty queen and some rich guy's daughter?" Her voice carried and a half dozen pairs of eyes turned in their direction.

Including a set of lovely gray eyes, the kind that saw through a man and left him wishing he was a better person.

"Do you need to shout?" he asked Charlie.

She arched a brow at him and smirked. "Why does it matter?"

"It just does," he said.

"She doesn't like you." Charlie finally had the sense to whisper.

"You need to stop now," he said in the best dad tone he knew. How in the world had his parents survived him and his brother?

"We're here," Charlie announced. "Where are the vegetables?"

Emery gave her a sharp look. "You're late. That means you stay ten minutes longer."

"It's his fault," Charlie argued.

"You're the one who had to change clothes three times," Beau reminded.

"Well, anyway, that isn't fair."

Emery didn't seem to care. "There are no vegetables, not yet. We're in the beginning stages of the garden. We've planted some seeds, but today we need to plant tomato, cucumber and pepper plants."

"Fine. Tell me what to do."

Beau shared a commiserating look with Emery. "How about we start with some respectful behavior?" he warned Charlie.

She appeared contrite.

"We're going to sit down for a minute, as a group, and share one area of our lives where we would like to improve." As Emery spoke, the group of six students made a collective groan. She merely shrugged and pointed them all to the table. "Grab a bottle of water, a sandwich, and have a seat."

They obeyed.

"What can I do to help?" Beau asked as they followed the group.

"You don't have to stay," she told him in her quiet way.

"If it isn't a problem, I would like to stay and help," he said. "I'm not staying because you need me here. Well, maybe a little. I'm staying because I think this is a worthwhile project."

"And you like worthwhile projects?" she asked. Her tone held no recrimination. She seemed curious. "Like mission trips to Africa?"

"Yes, I do. I've been blessed and I realize it isn't because I'm better or more valuable or deserving." He paused when she gave him a narrow-eyed look. "Once upon a time, I did feel that way about myself. I was a teenager, Emery. That person existed fifteen years ago, but he changed. I give back because I can and because it's what I'm called to do. I try very hard to live my faith. I spent a lot of years just attending church, as if that was the sum total of my relationship with God. Then, in college, I realized there was more to it than showing up on Sunday."

"I'm happy for you," she said. "I'm glad you're

this person now and I'm... I'm glad the girls have you."

What could he say to that? Nothing he said now would measure up to her words. Instead, he nodded toward the table of students and followed, allowing her to sit with them while he stood off to the side.

Emery addressed the students. "One thing that you would change about yourself or one thing you'd like to overcome. This table is our place for honesty. It is also not, definitely not, a place where we use words to hurt others."

"Anger," Charlie spoke into the silence. The word took everyone by surprise. She locked gazes with Emery. Cadence sat on her lap and Charlie hugged her sister tight. "I want to stop hating myself. I want to stop being so angry. I want to be forgiven."

She let out a breath, so harsh it seemed it had been pent up for weeks. Cadence hugged her neck and then whispered in Charlie's ear. Whatever it was left Charlie looking stricken. The other students sat in stunned silence.

Beau felt cold from the inside out, wanting to take the pain and whatever guilt Charlie felt about the tragedy that had taken the lives of her parents.

Emery cleared her throat. "Let's all write one word on a piece of paper. We'll put these words in a box in the center of the table. Each week when we come together, we're going to be thinking about the changes we need to make. The changes aren't for me, the school, your parents or the juvenile officer. These changes are for you to make a difference in your lives. Do this for yourselves."

"Let go and let God," Alex said. When Charlie gave him a look, he shrugged. "I'm not being mean. I know what Pastor Matthews said about letting God heal our wounds, but He can't if we hold on to them."

Charlie sat Cadence on the bench and got up. She looked like a wounded, frightened animal and Beau didn't know how to help her. As she started to walk away, Emery called out to her. Then she was up, grabbing her crutch and Zeb's leash.

"Could you show the kids how to plant the tomatoes? Nan is with Tilly." She had already started toward Charlie, Zeb at her side.

"I'll do my best," he said. "Unless you want me to go with Charlie."

"I've got this," she said. "The garden is about more than producing vegetables. It's about moments like this one. If we can teach the kids to communicate, to let people in, we can hopefully help them process and grow."

He watched her go and he knew, from the way

she leaned on her crutch, this wasn't a good day for her physically. He'd never realized how seriously her father had injured her. In a phone call with his mother the other day, she'd reminded him of the incident, something everyone in their small town had been aware of when it happened all of those years ago. Beau had been a young teen and hadn't paid a lot of attention to anything outside his realm of interest.

Emery had suffered with an untreated break that had left her with damage and infections that had taken months to treat. Plus several surgeries to save her leg—and her life.

Her father had only served two years in prison.

Refocusing back on the kids, he shoved his cowboy hat down on his head a little and shook off the need to take care of Emery. She did a pretty fine job of taking care of herself. Herself and everyone around her.

"Well, boss?" Alex spoke up, as he seemed to be fond of doing. Today he was a smiling teen with too-long blond hair and a bruise on his cheek that could have come from a mishap, or his father's fist. But this Alex wasn't the angry teen who had shoved Emery against the wall.

Beau had to hold back on the lecture he'd wanted to give the boy. Emery seemed to have forgiven and quickly moved on from the school incident. Beau doubted she'd want him to do anything other than stay quiet about what had happened.

"Tomato plants." He noticed they were in containers next to the garden. There were also strips of plastic and mulch. He'd never been a gardener, but there was a first time for everything.

As he started helping the students with the planting, he made a quick survey of the area, searching for Emery and Charlie. Cadence tugged at his shirt and pointed toward an old oak tree near the church. Charlie and Emery sat on a nearby bench.

"Caddie, I sure wish you'd talk to me and tell me how to help your sister."

Cadence sighed, but she didn't speak. Her eyes looked weepy and she continued to watch Emery and Charlie.

"Not happening today, is it?" Beau asked.

She looked up at him, but her lips remained clamped shut. He leaned down to hug her, then pulled her up in his arms and sat her on his shoulders, the way he'd seen her father do from time to time. She held on tight, giggling just a little.

He loved Cadence and Charlie. His heart filled up with the thought. He'd prayed hard on the flight home from Africa, praying he would do the right thing for them, praying God would give him the ability to love them the way their parents had intended, as a father.

God was answering, but man, it looked like they still had a rough road ahead of them. Healing would take time. It would take time to become a family, but there would always be two people missing from their lives. And maybe someday Beau would marry and give them a mother to love them.

His thoughts skipped to Emery and her place in their lives, as a friend, a mentor, someone they could lean on. Lately he'd caught himself thinking of her as he studied his Bible in the mornings, as he worked horses with Ethan and even as he drove to town delivering the girls to school. He thought about her when he had something on his mind, because he wondered what she would say if he told her.

He'd tried telling himself that Emery might be a friend. She'd definitely been a big help in getting the girls settled. She'd helped them to feel safe during the transition, from Nan's care to his.

He'd needed her help. He wasn't afraid to admit that.

But it took more than courage to admit that he might feel a little more for her than friendship. At his age, he ought to know what he was feeling for her.

A long time ago his dad had told him that a man knew he was in love when he couldn't get a woman out of his mind, and when it wasn't all about what she made him feel, but more about how he might make her happy, make her smile.

He shook his head, not wanting his mind to go down that path—yet.

In a little more than a week, he and the girls would leave Pleasant and head to Tulsa. Emery would no longer be a part of their daily lives.

Charlie and Cadence changed everything. For the first time, he had more to consider than himself. Whatever decisions he made about his life, his future, would impact the two little girls he'd been entrusted to raise.

The last thing he wanted to do was to hurt them. He also didn't want to hurt Emery, not this time around.

The future was no longer what he'd planned and he guessed it was more than two girls who had changed his path.

Chapter Nine

Emery sat next to Charlie on the wooden bench under the shade of an ancient oak with far-reaching branches. Zeb leaned against Charlie, giving comfort that a hurting child would accept. The girl had already shrugged away from Emery, avoiding her touch. Emery understood that need to maintain distance. She knew the fear of allowing touch, the fear of thinking if someone comforted her, she might fall apart and never be able to put herself back together.

She'd spent her childhood imagining herself as Humpty Dumpty.

It had taken two surgeons and multiple surgeries to somewhat put her physical body back together. The emotional part had taken a lot longer.

She sat for a moment, silently praying for

the right words. Before she could get them out, Charlie spoke.

"I hate myself," she admitted in a shaky voice, sounding younger than her fourteen years.

"Why?"

"I hate that I couldn't save my parents."

Emery's heart broke for the girl. "You have to share those thoughts, Charlie. You have to get them out."

"Yeah, that's what Mrs. Graves said, but..." She shook her head. "I don't want to talk about it. I don't want to relive that day."

"I get that," Emery sympathized. "I haven't been through what you've been through. I do know how it feels to be abandoned, without hope and alone. It takes time to overcome."

"Have you?" Charlie asked. "Overcome it, I mean?"

"I have. I do remember. Sometimes I have nightmares about it. But at the end of the day, I'm whole and happy with my life."

Silence fell over them, both lost in their own thoughts.

Across the lawn, Beau worked alongside the students as they planted tomatoes together. Cadence remained at his side.

"If he doesn't want us..." Charlie said. "I mean, he's not a dad. He didn't plan on having kids. He told my parents he'd take us, but that nothing would ever happen to them."

"He wants you," Emery assured the girl and prayed it was the truth.

"Caddie loves him. I know she still doesn't say much, but she wants to be with him all the time." Charlie looked down at her hands. "What if she forgets our mom and dad?"

"She won't. And we'll help her to remember. We have the photo albums from your home."

"No, I'm not ready to look at their faces." Charlie shook her head.

Nan and Tilly pulled up in Tilly's old boat of a Cadillac. The two women got out and joined the kids at the garden. Beau spoke to them, left Cadence with the women and started across the lawn in their direction.

As Beau drew closer, Emery felt a surprising wave of relief. His strength was evident, not merely physical but an emotional and spiritual strength that steadied the people around him.

He took a seat on the bench next to Emery, stretched his long legs and proceeded to relax as if they weren't sitting there in the throes of loss and heartache.

"Are you ready to join us?" he asked the teenager.

"You left Caddie," Charlie accused.

"She's with Nan and Tilly. I promise you she

is fine. So why don't we talk about your anger and hating yourself, because that seems like the most important thing to me right now."

"I don't want to talk about it," Charlie insisted, drawing her knees up to her chin. Zeb whined, climbed on the bench and curled up next to her.

"You weren't responsible," Emery said. "And you did the most important thing, you protected Cadence."

Tears streamed down Charlie's cheeks as if the dam had broken. She made a heartbreaking sound, then buried her face in her hands as sobs shook her body.

"It was my fault," she sobbed. "I made them late because I didn't want to go to the stupid dance recital. If only I'd gotten ready and helped Cadence find her dance costume, we wouldn't have been home. It was all my fault. My fault that they're dead and my fault that Cadence won't talk."

"Charlie…" Beau started, jumping up on his feet.

Charlie looked up at him. "See, now you hate me, too."

"No!" he said as he sank down to his haunches in front of her. "I do not hate you. Charlie, I love you and Cadence. Your parents loved you more than life, more than their lives. And you did exactly what they would have wanted. You kept your sister safe."

"She won't talk because I told her to stop being a crybaby. I told her to never talk, because if she talked, the men would hear us."

Emery felt cold from the inside out as she listened to the horror that the two girls had lived through.

Beau sat down next to Charlie and held her tight. Emery couldn't move as she prayed. Tears streaked down her cheeks and she brushed them away, wishing with all of her heart that she could take the pain away from Charlie and Cadence, and now from Beau.

After a few minutes, Charlie began to calm down. She remained close to Beau's side, in the safety of his arms. He stroked her hair and whispered, "I'm so sorry."

Emery finally managed to get some words out. "Charlie, honey, most adults couldn't handle or process what you lived through. You've been trying to process this by yourself. Opening up and talking about it today, it's so important for you and for Caddie."

"Her life is ruined because of me," Charlie said.

"No," Beau insisted. "She's alive because of you."

"Our parents…" Charlie whispered.

"Loved you," Beau answered. "They loved you."

"If I hadn't hidden in the closet like a coward…" She reached for Zeb and hugged the dog tight. "What if I could have done something?"

Emery remained silent, letting Beau take the lead. In the future, he would be the person Charlie and Cadence relied on.

"You weren't a coward." Beau pulled her close to his side. "You were brave and wonderful, even if it doesn't feel that way to you. Sometimes remaining silent is an act of courage."

They sat for a while, the three of them. Eventually Charlie let go of Zeb, wiped away her tears and sat up, as if she was done with her grieving. Emery hoped she was also on the road to healing, to forgiving herself.

"We should go back." Charlie sighed. "Caddie will be afraid if I'm not with her."

"Cadence is going to be okay," Emery assured her. "She's getting better every day."

"She needs to be in dance classes again," Charlie told them. "She loves to dance."

Beau nodded. "I'll find somewhere for her to go. What about you?"

"No, thanks, I just want to be a barrel racer." She glanced up at him. "We couldn't have horses when we lived in the city."

"No, I guess you couldn't."

Then suddenly Charlie got up and, with one backward glance at them, left to join the others.

"As if it never happened," Beau said after she was out of earshot.

"That's how I've always been, so I understand."

"Explain it for me, please?" he said as he reached for her hand.

She watched as he laced his fingers through hers and found that she didn't want to undo the connection.

"After an emotional moment like that one, revealing all of that pain, it helps to smile and pretend it didn't happen. She doesn't want to keep dwelling on it."

She reached for her crutch. As she made to push to her feet, pain seared a path down the muscles of her leg, from hip to ankle. She froze, trying to breathe past the ache that went deep. She closed her eyes and counted to ten, relaxing as she did.

"Let me help you." Beau's arm went around her waist.

Emery opened her eyes at the touch. The first thought that crossed her mind was to reject his help. The second was that pride truly did go before the fall and this fall could land her flat on her face.

"Thank you," she replied, humbled. "This

hasn't happened in a long time. I'll be fine in a minute."

"What's wrong?" he asked, clearly wanting to know.

"Muscle spasms." She took another deep breath and worked at relaxing. "I apologize for leaning on you, but I'm afraid I'm going to have to, just for a minute. I need to move, carefully."

"I'm yours to lean on," he said.

So she did, her right hand holding his arm as they made their way back to the garden. Her leg began to relax. Next week she would schedule a massage with her physical therapist. Tonight, she would drink Nan's chamomile and lavender tea.

"We're not leaving next week," he said nonchalantly as they crossed the yard.

The announcement brought her to a halt, still leaning most of her weight on him.

"Oh? Why is that?"

He grinned. "You want to get rid of me?"

"No, that's not it. I just wasn't aware of the change in plans. I mean, not that you have to inform me of your plans. Not that I have any say."

"I should have told you earlier," he offered. He moved closer to her side, sliding his arm around her waist and holding her as if she mattered.

She wanted to move from his embrace, but she couldn't, physically or emotionally.

"What made you change your mind? I thought you needed to get back to your home and work in Tulsa."

"The situation Charlie got herself into at school. They've asked that she stay in Pleasant for a month, working on the garden and meeting with Mrs. Graves twice a week."

"I think that's a good plan." The girls would have another month of stability before being uprooted. They could come up with a plan for making the transition easier. She told him that and he nodded in agreement.

In the meantime, Emery could find a way to keep her heart from being broken when they left. Because she would miss them. She told herself that Beau wasn't a part of that equation, but she'd never been one to lie, not even to herself.

Charlie squatted next to Cadence and showed her the best way to plant the peppers. The two remained close, as if their nearness kept them safe. Beau watched for a moment and then he joined in.

The other students had all left, even Alex. The teen's father hadn't shown up to get him, and he'd rejected the offer of a ride home, preferring to walk the short distance to the mobile home park where he lived. As he'd left, Alex had made comments to Emery that his dad was going to be mad if she kept sticking her nose in their business.

The comments had seemed more a warning than a threat, but it worried Beau nonetheless. Emery had a heart for helping kids and wanted to help them have better lives, even if it meant putting herself in harm's way.

"Can we get something to eat?" Charlie said as she stood up, stretching and glancing around. "Everyone is gone. Where's Nan and Tilly?"

He chuckled at the confused look on her face. "Alex just left. Nan and Tilly told you goodbye, but you were busy explaining to Cadence how the seeds you planted will sprout and grow."

"I love plants," she told him with a mischievous look. "I planned on being really angry about having to do this garden thing, but the truth is, I love to plant things and watch them grow."

"I'll make sure you have a big garden spot at my—our house in Tulsa."

"Is it in the city?" she asked. "I've gotten used to the country."

"It's outside the city. Plenty of land and animals."

"A horse?" she asked, her eyes darting past him.

He guessed that Emery must be on her way over to them.

"Is she okay?" Charlie asked.

"I think she will be," he said.

"Okay. So, I'm starving and I'm hot."

"We could go to Tilly's. After all, I think I owe Caddie a sundae, right?"

Charlie's eyes lit up.

Emery joined their little group, her car keys in her hand. "I'm going to head home now. Nan went back to Tilly's, and I think Avery will be picking her up for the evening and taking her to dinner."

"Then you don't have anything to do," Charlie said. "You can come with us."

"Charlie…" Beau warned.

"But she needs to eat, doesn't she?" Charlie said. "And we're getting sundaes."

"We're going to Tilly's," Beau mentioned. "I think what Charlie is trying to say is, 'Emery, would you like to go to Tilly's with us?'"

Charlie started to add more, but Beau shook his head to stop her. He noticed that she had hold of Zeb, as if the dog were her lifeline.

He felt hopeful. He wanted Emery to join them. More than that, he wanted her to *want* to join them.

"I should go home," she said. Her eyes softened to a warm gray when Cadence reached for her hand. "But I want an ice cream sundae more than I want to go home to fix myself a bowl of soup."

"You'll come with us?" Charlie asked.

"If Beau doesn't mind," she answered.

Beau most definitely didn't mind. "Do you want to meet us there or climb in the truck again?"

A sweet hint of a smile touched her mouth. "I think I would prefer my own car to climbing in that truck of yours."

"I can lift you up," he offered.

"No, thank you." She kissed Cadence on the forehead and then Charlie. She touched the teenager's chin, forcing her to look up. "Can Zeb ride with you? I know it's just a couple of blocks, but I think he enjoys truck rides."

Charlie looked to him for permission and he nodded. The girl grabbed the leash and clipped it on Zeb's harness. "Let's go, Zeb. Come on, Caddie, let's go get ice cream. Hey, we could just walk over there and then come back later for your truck. Couldn't we?"

"We can walk if you want to. Just don't get too far ahead of me."

"We'll stop at the end of the sidewalk," Charlie called back to him.

"Yeah," Cadence yelled.

They all briefly paused. Each syllable seemed like a gift that Cadence gave to them, each word a building block in her recovery. Beau thought about what Charlie had said, about telling Cadence she had to be quiet. She couldn't talk. She couldn't cry.

Fear of speaking, fear of what might happen should she speak. He realized the key was to show her she was safe. He would mention that to Mrs. Graves before the next session.

"I'm not walking," Emery said, still holding her keys. "I think that might be the last straw for me today."

"Understood," Beau said as he walked her to her car. "We'll meet you at the café."

They both stood there in the warm afternoon sunshine of late May. The girls were down the sidewalk, but Charlie's voice drifted back. She was telling Cadence something about a song they used to sing together.

His gaze slid to the woman standing at his side and he realized his hand had moved to her hair, where the silky strands slipped between his fingers, releasing the herbal scent of her shampoo. It was broad daylight, he reminded himself. Plus, the kids were nearby.

He hesitated for a moment, giving her a chance to tell him to back off. She didn't. So he kissed her softly, gently, only a few stolen seconds on a spring afternoon, but enough to change everything he'd ever thought about his future.

After he pulled away, he opened her car door and she slid behind the wheel. She started to speak, but he shook his head. "Not yet," he said.

"Beau," she started again.

"Meet you at Tilly's." He gently closed her door, smiling at the look she gave him through the rolled-up window, half exasperation and half dreamy-eyed.

He hurried to catch up with the girls.

When he and the girls walked through the door of the café, they were greeted by the tinkle of the bell, cool air and a few gruff hellos from the gossip table, as Tilly called it. The three tables pushed together stretched along the front window of the café and rarely did anyone sit there other than a group of local farmers. Their ages ranged from midthirties to mideighties. Some wore bib overalls, and plaid shirts, others new blue jeans and shiny boots. They preferred that front window where they could see who came and went and what happened on the street.

Junior McDonald pushed back the fishing cap he always wore and gave them a long and assessing look. "Beau Wilde, you're still in town. You thinking about settling back in Pleasant?"

"Haven't really considered it, Junior. I've got my own place."

Dan Townsend chuckled. "Well, that job must not need you too much if you don't have to be there."

"That's the wonder of technology," Beau told the man who managed the local bank. "You know that, Dan. Computers and the internet keep us connected to everyone, all the time."

Dan raised his coffee cup in salute. "I guess you got me there." He winked. "Emery joining you?"

"Yeah, she's going to join us."

Dan had switched his attention to the front door, where Emery stood, appearing to be gathering her courage before facing the crowd. He understood that look, felt it to the depth of his being. Being seen together in this small town meant people would assume a relationship, even if there wasn't one.

Friendship. He'd label what was developing between them as friendship, even if it felt a little trickier than that. It felt as if he were on the verge of something new. It made his heart speed up a little as he thought about her, about this new life he'd just inherited.

But there was nowhere he'd rather be than with Charlie and Cadence, listening to them order sundaes for lunch, seeing Tilly laugh at their antics and waiting for Emery to walk through the door to join them.

Nowhere in the world he would rather be, he repeated to himself. He wanted to be here. With Emery. Because friendship wasn't really the right word for what he felt.

Chapter Ten

First days. It had been five days since the kiss.

As she left school on Thursday, it was the kiss that had her preoccupied. She'd obviously been kissed before. She was almost thirty. She'd dated. But never before had a simple kiss upset the balance of her life.

With the kiss came the old thoughts, the ones she'd tried to banish over the years. Did he have an agenda? Did he just feel sorry for her? Would he come to regret the kiss?

She had to stop.

She loved Jesus, but she was still a frail and flawed human being who sometimes carried big doubts and old wounds.

"Emery!"

She turned at the voice and saw Charlie standing at the edge of the sidewalk, Cadence's hand in hers. She'd forgotten them! Forgotten that she'd promised to take them home. She'd been so distracted by... Well, she wasn't going to think about it anymore. She would not think about Beau, or about how odd it felt deep inside where trust might possibly be growing. She trusted him. Trust was reserved for those closest to her, to Nan, to her sisters, to her closest friends. If she trusted, would he hurt her?

And again, he'd stolen his way into her thoughts.

She hurried over to the girls, Zeb at her side, giving her serious questioning looks.

"Don't look at me like that," she whispered.

His next look bordered on accusing.

"I'm so sorry. I was distracted and forgot." She shrugged.

"Sure, it's okay." Charlie kept hold of Cadence.

"It isn't okay," she told the teenager. "But thank you for being so understanding."

Emery smiled down at Cadence. The little girl was bouncy and a smile filled her face.

"What's up with you, Caddie girl?"

"Chickens," Charlie answered. "We have chickens and one is a silkie. It's tiny and likes to be held."

"That sounds like fun," Emery said. The look Charlie gave her guaranteed she didn't sound nearly as enthusiastic as the girl thought she should.

Cadence wrapped her hand around Zeb's collar and took a step.

"Right, we should go," Emery agreed. She kept a tight hold on Zeb's leash as they crossed the blacktop to her car. And Cadence kept a tight hand on Zeb's harness. "Cadence, did you have a good day in school?"

Cadence gave her a not-really-happy look.

"That good, huh?" Emery asked. "Did you play with friends?"

Cadence looked away.

"Ah," Emery said softly.

"What happened to your car!" Charlie shouted, letting go of Cadence's hand to point. "Emery, your car!"

"I see," Emery said. "Calm down."

Sensing their distress, Zeb whined and moved closer to the girls.

Words, pretty bad words, the kind she hoped Cadence couldn't read, were keyed into the paint of her car. Most of the damage was on the side that faced away from the school. And she'd parked in the side lot where there were no cameras. Whoever had done this to her car, they'd paid attention and knew how to keep from being detected.

"How can you be so calm?" Charlie asked. "Someone ruined your car!"

"I know," Emery said. Truthfully, she wasn't calm. She felt her insides quake at the thought that someone had been able to do this. Someone who obviously had a real grievance against her. She worked with troubled teens. She often made calls to the state to report suspected child abuse. Any number of people might have wanted to get back at her.

When the police arrived a short time later, she tried to think of names of people who might be angry with her, but how would they ever prove who had vandalized her car if no one reported seeing it happen?

An hour later when they pulled up to the Rocking W, she still couldn't take a real breath without feeling shaky. The trip to the ranch from town had been a quiet one. Even normally chatty Charlie had remained silent.

As they got out of the car, the girl spotted the chickens in the fenced-in coop and her smile returned. She hurried to unbuckle Cadence and then she pulled her onto her back and gave her a piggyback ride to the chickens.

"Is that a rooster I see?" Emery asked as the three of them, four counting Zeb, approached the chicken pen.

"Yeah, his name is Lee." Charlie opened the

door to the pen. "Uncle Ethan let us pick our chickens. The lady we got them from said she named the rooster after her husband because he's always crowing about something."

Charlie and Cadence checked for eggs, then Charlie cleaned the waterer, dumping the dirty water and letting the lid refill with fresh. The chickens hurried forward to drink. The girls slipped back out of the pen and latched the door. The entire time, Zeb wiggled his excitement over the new additions to the Rocking W.

"Lee the rooster crows all the time."

Charlie gave Emery a look, obviously expecting a reaction to the rooster story.

Emery did her best to laugh, but her heart wasn't in it. She was still thinking about her car and whoever had done the damage.

"Are you okay?" Charlie asked, her voice quiet and unsure.

"I'm good." Emery handed Zeb's leash to Cadence, causing the girl to smile big. When Emery hugged Charlie close, the teen stiffened, then relaxed into the embrace. "We're all good."

"I know," Charlie sniffled against her shoulder. "It just makes me mad."

"And a little bit afraid," Emery suggested as she released the girl.

"Yeah, kind of. For you."

"I'm safe," Emery assured her. "And so are you."

She hoped the words were the truth. For all of their sakes.

"There's Beau," Charlie said, her voice taking on an excitedness that took Emery by surprise. "He's back from Tulsa."

Emery watched the truck pull into the garage. Beau was home. Something deep within her crumbled at the sight of him. All of the stress the week had caused, the damage to her car, all of it rolled together and she needed…him. She needed his quiet strength, his presence.

On top of that, she wanted to discuss the job offer with him. She wanted to ask him what he thought about her leaving Pleasant. That thought took her aback. She'd been consumed with guilt because she'd been seriously considering taking the position. It was the type of job she'd always wanted.

But every time she considered accepting the job, she thought of Nan. Nan needed her.

Cadence grabbed Emery's hand and tugged her toward the house. She went, Zeb trotting next to them, his tail wagging a greeting.

Beau met them in the yard and Emery slowed at his approach. He looked the part of a businessman in his button-down shirt and tie. His hair had been trimmed, and he'd shaved. Cadence broke free and ran to him. Emery remained planted in one spot, watching as he lifted the child and tossed her in the air.

"Caddie, you're a sight for sore eyes. I only stayed one night in Tulsa, but it felt like forever." He settled the little girl in his arms and then reached for Charlie, pulling her into a hug. "Charlie, did you hold down the fort while I was gone?"

"Kind of," she said with a sheepish grin and a shrug. "Uncle Ethan is saddling True for my riding lesson, plus he got a pony for Caddie. And someone messed up Emery's car. Bad."

"They what?" His focus was now on Emery and she could have done without that.

"It's nothing," she stated, hoping he would believe what she didn't.

"It isn't nothing. They keyed her car and wrote bad names on the side."

"When did this happen?" he asked, his voice gruff, his dark eyes capturing hers.

"We discovered it after school today." Emery really wished he would let it go. She didn't want to discuss it. She definitely didn't want to continue the discussion in front of the girls.

"You called the police?" he asked.

"I called the police," she said, while giving the girls a pointed look.

He brushed his fingers through his hair. That

was when Charlie reached for Cadence. Her gaze swung between them, a tiny frown marring her expression.

"Caddie and I are going to help Uncle Ethan."

"You don't have to go," Emery said to Charlie's retreating back. Slowly she circled back around to the man who still wanted answers to his questions.

"Are you okay?" he asked, stepping closer.

"I'm good. It was nothing, just some kid playing a prank that went too far."

A light breeze kicked up and the mountain-air scent of his cologne teased her senses. She was almost thirty, and for the first time in forever, she truly wanted to step close to a man, let him hold her and just feel safe, feel...

Her heart and brain were in a real duel because her brain reminded her how it felt to trust and be hurt. Just once she'd like to be the person who took a chance, who stepped out on a limb and didn't fear the fall.

"How do you know it was a kid?" he asked.

She didn't know for sure, but she hoped. She shrugged, not really having an answer.

"What did the police say?"

"To be careful," she said. "They don't have answers. They took pictures, asked questions. That's really all that they can do."

"This worries me," he told her, his voice tight, making his concern real.

"You don't have to worry about me," she said. "I can take care of myself."

All of her life she'd only ever relied on God, herself and Nan. She didn't know how Beau had worked his way into that circle. Earlier that day during her lunch break she'd thought about him, thought about asking his opinion on the new job offer.

"Emery?"

She looked up, into troubled dark eyes.

"I'm sure you can take care of yourself, but…"

"But?" She regretted the word. It made her feel as if she were baiting him, trying to get him to say more than he'd intended.

"I don't want you to get hurt," he said. And then his arms were around her and he held her close, his lips brushing the top of her head.

Standing there in his arms was the last place she ever expected to be. At the moment, she almost wanted him to never let go.

But he would. He would take the girls and go back to his life in Oklahoma. He would forget about her. She wasn't the woman a man wanted to date. She was the woman they felt sorry for.

For a moment she got to be someone else, someone treasured. Abruptly she pulled away from him, telling herself that what she'd felt was nothing more than vulnerability. With so much going on, so many changes taking place, she'd needed someone to lean on right now.

That had to be the reason she'd felt so safe in his arms.

After just two days away, Beau hadn't planned on such a homecoming. He'd been surprised when he walked out of the garage to see Charlie and Cadence hurtling toward him, smiles on their faces. No doubt they were still grieving, but they were also starting to heal.

Two months ago, he wouldn't have thought that this would be his life. But life changes in the blink of an eye. He knew it would take time for them all to adjust, but he'd learned something—he'd been lonely. He'd been so busy running the business, keeping all of the balls in the air from dropping, he hadn't taken time for family.

He'd missed his hometown, the Rocking W, his brother. He'd missed daily talks with his parents.

The biggest surprise was, he'd missed a woman he hadn't really known.

How could something as simple as having her in his arms be the greatest gift he'd ever been given? Everything about Emery Guthrie took him by surprise.

"The girls have missed you," she said as she pulled free. The subject of the girls was safe. She obviously wanted to get them back on neutral footing and out of the dangerous territory of emotions.

She didn't trust him. He knew that and was trying to rectify it. But it wouldn't happen overnight.

"I missed them, too," he told her. "While I was in Tulsa, I contacted an interior decorator. The girls are going to need their own room at my house. I also called a friend who might be able to help me find a housekeeper."

She made a face.

"What?" he asked.

She clamped her lips and shook her head. "Sorry, it's none of my business."

"Too late, you already made it your business."

She let out a long sigh. "Please don't let a housekeeper raise them. Also, include them in the decorating process. They'll want to make the room their own."

"You're right, I'll have them talk to the decorator. They can either have their own rooms or share. Don't worry, I promise I'm raising these girls, not the housekeeper. I just need help on busy days, and someone to cook for us. I want them to have real meals. Not fast food all the time." He winked at her.

"They'll appreciate that." Her gray eyes sparkled.

He glanced past her. "Am I seeing chickens and ducks over there or is that my imagination?"

She laughed, the sound sweet and contagious. "Your brother bought them for the girls. Hens, ducks and a rooster named Lee."

"I hope he doesn't expect me to take them with me to Tulsa."

"I think the girls might get attached to them and expect to move them."

"Would you consider making a few trips to Tulsa?" Beau asked as they stood there watching the hens. "I think it might help the girls if you're there with us as we get settled in. It might make them more comfortable with the process."

She didn't answer right away. He glanced her way, loving the thoughtful expression on her face as she considered her answer. He wanted her to say yes, as much for himself as for the girls.

The idea of missing her took him by surprise.

"Please say yes," he said with a grin, a hopeful bit of humor.

"I love spending time with the girls…and with you." She said it hesitantly and he doubted she wanted to include him in that statement.

"I'm not sure if it's a good idea for me to go with you to Tulsa. I don't want the girls to see us as a couple. Also…"

He waited for her to finish because he guessed what came next would be about him.

She didn't finish.

"Also?" he prodded.

"Nothing, really. I just…" She sighed. "When you go back to Tulsa, it will be the three of you. They need to get used to that."

Temporary. She only planned to be in their lives temporarily. Of course, that made sense. What she'd said, her reason for not joining them on a trip to Tulsa, that also made sense. What didn't make sense was the way it felt, to think that she wouldn't be in their lives.

He didn't want to think about life in Tulsa when it would just be the three of them. Without Emery. The sooner they adjusted, she seemed to be saying, the better.

"I get why you think it would be a bad idea. But I think my plan also has merit."

"I'm sure you do," she said, not looking at him. But then, as if she wasn't in control of the gesture, her right hand came up, touching his shoulder. She seemed to suddenly realize what she'd done and she pretended to dust an invisible fleck of something off his shirt.

"Yes, I do think my plan has merit," he managed to say while distracted by thoughts of kissing her. "If you're with us, even for day trips to Tulsa, the girls will have you there, helping them to adjust."

"I'll think about it," she agreed. Her right hand was now fisted at her side, as if she meant to keep it tightly in control.

He smiled and she surprised him by doing the same. He'd never felt butterflies in any situation with a woman, not butterflies of this level, brought on by something so simple.

"Why are you looking at me like that?" she asked.

"Because you smiled and it always catches me off guard. In a good way."

She backed away from him, the smile disappearing. "I should go."

"Stay," he said. "Please. The girls are going to show off their riding skills."

To prove his point, voices carried from the small arena Ethan had constructed when he'd started doing more serious horse training. They watched as Charlie led a black horse, True, around the large rectangle. Cadence, still clutching Zeb's leash, stood outside the white vinyl fence watching.

"Nan is expecting me home," Emery told him, her gaze lingering on Charlie and her horse. "I used to dream of riding."

"We have plenty of horses," he said a little too hopefully. "We could go riding."

She lifted her crutch. "This makes it difficult. I have muscle spasms and…it isn't worth discussing."

"It is worth discussing," he told her, wanting to know her heartache, her dreams… He wanted to know her.

She moved quickly, coming to her tiptoes and kissing his cheek. "I have to go."

He was too stunned to move. When he came back to his senses, she was already a dozen feet away.

"I'll walk you to your car."

"You really don't need…"

He caught up with her. "I do need to."

He'd never wanted a woman's smile the way he wanted hers. The kind of smile that was meant just for him, because she thought he was funny or she was glad to see him. All of his life, women had chased him. He hadn't enjoyed the chase, not since high school. He wanted a woman who loved him for himself and not a woman who merely wanted to "catch" him.

He wanted a woman who would be his partner in life. And every time he looked at Emery, he thought here was a woman he wanted to share his life with.

Chapter Eleven

Saturday morning Emery woke to bright blue skies and a cool breeze blowing in her window. She glanced at her watch and groaned. She hadn't meant to sleep so late. She had to be at the garden by ten. They'd decided to get an early start, before it got hot. Now she regretted that decision.

What she really wanted was to sleep another hour and celebrate the fact that school was out for the summer. She closed her eyes, anticipating a few more minutes of sleep, but her eyes opened wide as she remembered the dream. She'd been with Beau and the girls, walking near the river. Beau had called her "honey."

Zeb moved from the foot of the bed and crawled up to sleep next to her.

"Come on, lazy dog. Time for us to get up and get moving." She rubbed his ears and he groaned and rolled over on his back for a belly rub. She loved her dog. Not only for herself, but for what he meant to so many children and adults. He probably didn't understand how much comfort he gave, he did it so instinctually. She wished more people could have the compassion Zeb had for humans.

Fifteen minutes later he followed her down the stairs. She'd put his harness on him, but she carried his leash in her purse. The smell of coffee and something sweet greeted them as they walked through the house to the kitchen.

Clara and Nan sat at the kitchen table, a book open in front of them. The two were discussing pictures that had been taped next to the notes Nan had made. The scrapbook was meant to help Nan with her memory for as long as possible.

"Good morning," Emery said as she entered the room.

"Oh, goodness, I didn't notice you were here." Nan pushed a plate of muffins across the table.

"I know. You were deep in thought." Emery grabbed a chocolate chip muffin and put it on a plate. "They smell delicious."

"They are delicious," Clara said as she grabbed another.

"I'll see for myself," Emery said. "Where's Grace?"

Clara's baby girl had stolen all of their hearts.

"She's with her daddy," Clara said. By daddy, she meant Tucker Church, her husband. He was the only father Grace would ever know and he was the best.

Nan tapped the book. "I know you girls think this memory book is a good idea. But it's also causing me to feel a little melancholy, all of these stories of my life, all of the memories of my past and the people I loved. Reminds me of a song. I'm kind of homesick for heaven. I've never been, but the people I love are there."

Emery refrained from reminding Nan that she had people on this side of heaven who loved her, too. The words weren't necessary, Nan knew and Emery believed that even if she forgot their names, their stories, she would remember their love.

She brought the conversation back to Nan's stories of the past.

"I love the river stories," Emery said as she poured herself a cup of coffee from the carafe. "The photographs you've found tell the story of when this river of ours attracted people from across the world."

"Yes, the past. It's all in this journal and in here." Nan tapped her head. "It's my todays that are a bit fuzzy. I hate forgetting names and I really don't like getting lost in my own town."

"I know." Emery covered Nan's hand with her own.

"Oh, girls, you are all so precious to me. Please keep my boat shop going. I want to believe that in one hundred years, we'll still have our people floating this river, keeping it healthy and peaceful."

"I'll do my very best," Emery promised. Clara echoed the sentiment. The two shared a look, both blinking to keep tears from falling.

"And all these stories, they'll become yours." Nan pushed back from the table and walked to the kitchen sink, where she stood for several minutes, her back to them as she fought for control.

"I'm thankful for all that you've written in that book." Clara joined Nan at the sink, wrapping an arm around her waist and pulling her close. "It should be a novel. The idea that at one time your grandfather ran a river outfitter that took famous people on float trips."

"It was a different time," Nan said. "Movie stars with big hats and fancy dresses sitting at the front of a johnboat made by my grandfather while he paddled them downriver. They would catch fish and he would fry them up for dinner. It was a different time, when there wasn't a lake. It was all river."

Nan returned to her seat at the table.

"I wouldn't mind that time," Emery said. "It was much simpler."

"Like today, there was good and bad. Life was simple, but folks had to work hard to make ends meet. They didn't have all of our conveniences." Nan smiled up from the photos. "Thank you for taking that little journey with me, Avery. I'm so glad you're here with me. However, I do think that someday you'll get married. That seems to be the reason God is sending my girls home, to get you married off."

"I don't think that's my reason for being home," Emery said, not bothering to correct Nan with the right name. It wasn't important. What was important was that Nan stayed with them for as long as possible. "I'm happy to stay here with you."

"What about Beau Wilde?" Nan grinned as she asked, then ducked her head and pretended to study photos from a century ago.

"He's a friend. That's all."

Clara gave her a look. "Really? Friend?"

"Just a friend. Barely," Emery clarified. "I need to go soon. I have to be at the community garden by ten."

"Hmm," said Nan. She glanced up at her kitchen clock. "What time do you have to leave?"

"In fifteen minutes."

"I think I'll sit this one out. As a matter of

fact, I'm going to go get ready. I think we're having a ladies' meeting at church. Emery, I do worry about you. I don't think you've allowed yourself to get close to anyone because you're worried about what a serious relationship would mean."

"Nan," Emery objected, but Nan held up a hand.

"I'm not going to be hushed," Nan told her. "We should have talked about this a long time ago. Fourteen years ago, actually. See how well I remember? When they did that surgery and told you that you might never have children, I was so angry. You were too young to have so much piled on your shoulders."

"It was better to know the truth and deal with it." Emery avoided looking at Clara, because she didn't want to see the shock Nan's announcement would have elicited.

"I suppose you're right." Nan reached for her hand. "I had a dozen girls and loved every one of you as my own. Just remember that."

"We loved you right back. I know that I was almost eighteen when we finalized the adoption, but I'm thankful every day that you're my mom."

Nan patted her hand and a tear dropped on the table, possibly Nan's and maybe Emery's. Clara had moved away, but Emery saw her swipe a hand across her cheek.

"Okay, you should go. And take that dog of yours. He's getting under my feet and making a nuisance of himself."

"I'd rather leave him," Emery said.

Nan shook her head. "Stop being a worrier."

"I'll try." She kissed Nan on the cheek, hugged Clara and headed out the door.

Zeb rode next to her on the way to town. As soon as they pulled into the church parking lot, he began to wiggle and wag his tail. He could see the students at the garden. Beau was also there with Cadence and Charlie. She drew in a breath, fortifying herself.

Only, it was no longer fear or anger that she had to protect her heart against. He'd done what he intended. He'd proved to her that he'd changed. That might hurt as badly as knowing him from the past, only in a different way.

As she got out of her car, she noticed the activity around the garden seemed frenzied and upset. They hadn't used pesticides, and she hoped that hadn't been a mistake. She made the painfully long walk across the yard, using both crutches today, as her doctor had recommended, to give her joints and muscles a rest for a few weeks.

She had come to terms with this part of her

life, realizing ten years ago that it was only a portion of who she was. She was *not* a disability. She had many abilities. She had one leg that sometimes caused her problems, but she could deal with it.

Beau spotted her and she immediately saw his concern. She frowned when he left the group and hurried her way.

"Get that look off your face or turn around and go back the way you came." She tried for a light tone, hoping to ease the awkwardness of the moment.

He drew in a breath, blinked and fake smiled. "How's this?"

"Not good."

He tried a cheesier smile and she laughed. "That's even worse."

"But you laughed."

No one had ever worked so hard at making her smile.

"You're a dork, so laughter was a natural response to that dorkiness." She smiled.

"So, how's your Saturday?" he asked as he walked next to her.

"Fine. Why are you acting this way?"

"What way?"

"Suspicious."

"Are you okay?" he asked, sidestepping her concerns.

"I'm fine. This is one of those odd times when I've overdone it and I need to give my body a break."

"Okay," he said, as if processing. "I worry that we're the reason you overdo things."

"You're not," she insisted. "So, why are the kids upset and where is Alex?"

"Ah, yes, classic move. Changing the subject."

"I answered you."

"Yes, you did. About the kids… There's been some vandalism here."

"And you didn't tell me?" She quickened her pace, fighting the pain that it caused.

"I would have told you, but I was distracted by concern for you, which does seem more important than tomato plants at the moment."

"I'm used to my pain, so it needn't worry you. What happened to the garden?"

"The fencing has been knocked down and some of our plants uprooted."

"Oh no," she said, startled by the damage she could now see. "Why would anyone do this?"

"That's what we want to know," Jarod said with all of the outrage a fifteen-year-old could muster. Jarod was a repeat juvenile offender. This program seemed to be what he needed. He'd taken great pride in the garden. Now it was all a mess and Jarod was understandably furious.

"If I find out that Alex did this…" the teen said with a growl.

"We're not going to accuse anyone, not without proof." Emery stopped at the edge of the garden to survey the damage. Zeb pulled at his leash and she released him. He went immediately to Charlie. The girl stood at the edge of the garden of destruction, a single tear tracing a path down her cheek.

"Gardens are stupid," she said.

"Gardens aren't stupid," Beau told her as he went to put an arm around her. Zeb sat next to her, licking her hand. She gave him a loving pat on the top of his head. "Gardens can be replanted."

"But everyone worked so hard. Emery said the spinach and lettuce would have been ready next week."

Jarod picked up a tomato plant that had been uprooted and tried to replant it. It hurt Emery's heart to see the tall and lanky boy, a little awkward, kneeling on the ground with the spindly plant cupped between his hands.

"It's going to be okay," Emery told her small gardening squad. "We'll figure this out, but we will also replant."

Nan's needlepoint verse came to mind. *In*

all these things we are more than conquerors through Him that loved us.

Even in this? She looked heavenward and prayed for the right words to say to this group of teens.

"As much as this hurts," she told them, "we're going to be okay. This is a temporary setback, as are so many things in life. So we focus on moving forward and the goals we've made. We can't let this discourage us or we're letting who-ever did this win."

"I hate whoever did this," said Jennifer, an older teen.

Emery responded, "Yes, we're angry with the person who did this, but we won't hold on to that anger."

"Ugh, stop." Jarod stood up and backed away carefully from the garden and the freshly re-planted tomato. "Whoever did this is probably the same one that messed up your car. You forgive that?"

"I do," she said gently. "I've learned that hold-ing on to anger keeps us anchored to the past."

She ignored Beau, because her statement went beyond their shared past. Her road of for-giving those who had hurt her had been long and sometimes difficult. There had been nu-merous players and she'd worked through the pain of letting go.

Several trucks pulled into the church parking lot, as well as an SUV with a county sheriff decal on the driver's side door. Pastor Matthews got out of one truck and he waited for the officer to join him before heading in the direction of the garden. The other men were gathering tools and equipment from their truck beds before taking off in the direction of the church.

"Did you call the police?" Emery asked Beau as she casually studied the men.

"I did. I also let Pastor Matthews know. In case he wanted to check the church for damage."

"I'll talk to them," Beau offered. Then he seemed to think better of that idea. "If you want."

She felt the corners of her mouth tugging upward. "Yes, please. Since you asked so nicely."

"Can Caddie stay with you?"

"Of course," she answered. It seemed a fair trade. She would watch Cadence and he could do the talking.

She watched as he talked to Pastor Matthews and the police officer. Notes were jotted down. Pictures were taken. The kids had all gathered to give their account of things. The officer shook his head, disagreeing with something Jarod Black said to him.

She guessed Jarod thought Alex Little was responsible.

Amy, new to the program, joined Emery.

"Do you think they'll do it again?" Amy asked, waving her hand at the garden. "It seems like a lot of work just to have someone keep messing it up."

"I hope they won't." Emery pointed to a nearby bench. "Let's sit."

"Okay. I'm sorry." Amy held a hand out to Cadence. "I don't mean to be negative. My dad says that's what my problem is. I never see the good in things."

"I understand," Emery told the girl. "When the bad is all around us, it kind of becomes overwhelming and takes all of our attention. Sometimes we have to look a little harder for the good. But the good of this garden, even if it gets vandalized, even if the plants die, is that we're here together, growing friendships and learning to make good decisions that will help us our entire lives."

Amy sat down next to her.

"I guess you're right."

"I know I'm right," Emery said with a wink.

Across the lawn, the meeting seemed to end. The police officer shook hands with Beau and Pastor Matthews, spoke to the students and left.

Emery remained on the bench with Cadence cuddled close, possibly dozing in the early June sunshine. For a minute, maybe two, Emery considered that she should get up. She should take charge of her group. It definitely shouldn't be Beau as she sat by and watched. What a strange feeling, to sit back and willingly let him take this load.

Her heart did a funny stutter that felt a lot like Beau's truck had the day she'd driven it.

She'd just been telling Amy about a lesson in growing and learning. As Emery glanced in the direction of Beau Wilde, she felt as if God was teaching her the same lesson. And if she made it all about a lesson, not her heart, that made her feel better about the relationship.

Beau was in her life for a season to help her forgive, to teach her to let others help. In a few weeks, he would leave and they would both go on with their separate lives, but they would be forever changed by this time together.

A flash of something crossed Emery's face and softened her expression. Beau wanted to go to her, ask her what had brought on that thoughtful look. Instead, he directed Pastor Matthews and Harold Spencer, owner of the Farm and Home store, to set the boxes they carried next to the garden.

After the officer had left, the two men had gathered up garden supplies from the backs of their trucks. A surprise for the youth.

Although Beau had lived away from Pleasant for all of his adult life, this small town and its generosity never ceased to amaze him.

"Tomato plants, broccoli, peppers and watermelon," Pastor Matthews told the students, who had gathered around to see what he'd brought. "Now, I plan on getting at least one of those watermelons come harvest time."

"I'm real proud of you kids and what you're doing here. I decided you should have a reward for your hard work. When you get finished up here, you go order lunch from Tilly. She'll charge it to my account." Harold Spencer made eye contact with each of the kids. The farm store owner was big and gruff, but a good man.

They thanked him. The boys even stepped forward to shake his hand. Beau saw then that Emery was making a difference. A few hours a week, some seeds planted, both in the ground and in the hearts of these kids and lives were potentially changed.

Emery now had her group gathered together and they were making a plan for the new plants. Cadence held tight to her hand, staying in the middle of the excitement. Emery truly had a way with these kids.

Another reason to love her.

Love. He choked on that thought. He'd had

plenty of girlfriends in high school and college. He'd dated as an adult and he'd even thought he was in love. This moment shined a light on how wrong he'd been about love and what it would feel like to fall.

"Are you sick?" Charlie appeared at his side.

"Not at all. Just thinking about the garden."

"Sure," she said. "Because the garden is standing over there."

It was the truth. He was thinking about the garden, the garden caretaker and the obvious problem he faced going forward.

Fortunately, the work had begun. Emery was talking to Cadence as the others began the jobs she'd assigned them. He moved closer to hear what she was saying.

"Your job is going to be planting lettuce. I have a spot over here in the corner of the garden that is going to be all yours. Would you like to try planting carrots, too? They don't always do well in this rocky soil, but you might get small ones."

Cadence took the seed packet and followed Emery. Beau did the same. He couldn't help himself. He watched as she showed the littlest helper how to dig tiny holes, insert the seed and cover loosely with just the right amount of soil.

The two worked together with Emery sitting

on the ground, her legs stretched out in front of her, Cadence squatted next to her. They created such a beautiful picture, Emery with her dark hair, leaning to watch, Cadence with her strawberry blond curls and her pixie face, happily digging in the dirt.

Emery glanced up at him, her brow furrowing. "What are you staring at?"

"The two of you."

"You should stop now," she said with a hint of a smile. "And help me up."

"Oh, of course, Your Highness." He moved to her side and she reached up with both hands.

He took her hands in his, and for a moment, neither of them moved. Beau wasn't sure what he should say, but he guessed that anything he said would be unwelcome. The wariness still lingered in her eyes, even if it was mixed with a healthy dose of confusion. Slowly he pulled her to her feet, holding her for a minute as she got her balance.

"Awkward," Charlie called out to them.

He let go, her fingers slipping from his and he and handed her the crutches she'd left on the ground. She didn't look at him as she steadied herself on the cushioned handles. A hint of pink touched her cheeks.

Now or never, the phrase stuck in his mind.

"Emery, I don't want to lose you when we leave."

"I'm sorry?" She went from slightly pink to pale.

Maybe he should have gone with never.

She wouldn't make eye contact with him and he desperately wanted her to look up.

"You're special to me, to the girls. I can't imagine not having your presence in our lives." He swiped a hand over his face. "I'm not sure what I'm trying to say. Except this, please stay in our lives."

"I love Cadence and Charlie. I want the very best for them."

"I know you do." He felt strangely unhinged, wishing he could convince her to make him a part of her circle.

"I'll visit. I'll make sure they feel settled." There was a catch in her voice.

"You are a very important part of their lives, of *our* lives."

She gave him one of her long, serious looks. "That's sweet of you to say, but we both know how this will end."

"How will it end?"

"We'll make plans to get together, for the girls. For a while we will even do it. Life will soon begin to interfere. Work, school, activities. It will be okay, because that will mean the girls are settled and feeling secure. It will mean that you've adjusted and are doing your best with them."

"Then we should make sure it doesn't happen that way."

Cadence had left her little plot of soil and she now sat next to Charlie, leaning in close as if Charlie was her security in this strange world she'd been thrust into.

"At some point, we need to release Charlie from her role of caretaker." Emery studied the two girls as she spoke. "I know that Charlie wants to take care of her sister. I know that Cadence needs her big sister, but Charlie needs to be able to find some semblance of normal, of life before…" She didn't finish. "I'm afraid she'll let her guilt consume her and she'll spend her life trying to make it up to Cadence."

"I'll watch them, Emery. I'll make sure they're okay."

She flicked away a tear and nodded. "I know you will."

"I'm not ready for you to exit our lives yet, Emery."

She gave him a questioning look, as if she didn't know what to make of that statement. He didn't know what to tell her.

"But we will exit each other's lives," she said softly, keeping the conversation between them.

"I've been offered a job at a residential facility near St. Louis. Next year I'll have completed my doctorate, I hope, and this is my dream job."

"But…?" He could hear the questions, the doubts in her voice. He hoped she didn't notice how her announcement gutted him, made him feel as if she would slip away from them.

"Nan," she said simply. "I can't leave Nan."

"I think she wouldn't want to be the one standing between you and a job you've always wanted."

"I know." She walked away from the garden and he followed. "I'm sorry, I didn't mean to dump this on you. I haven't talked to anyone about the job offer and I needed to."

"It's a big decision."

"I know. And I'm praying about it. It's just… They want me to make a decision and it isn't that simple. I love my job here. I love the students. I love my family."

"But you went to school planning for something more."

"Yes," she agreed. She tilted her head to look up at him. "Thank you for letting me talk. I'm working on being able to confide in people."

"And you picked me to practice on?" He found the humor in that.

She laughed a little. "Yes. Ironic, isn't it?"

It made him hopeful. But hope was quickly replaced by something that felt more like loss.

He and the girls would be moving to Tulsa soon. Emery might take a job that would put six hours between them. When he'd started this journey, he'd never expected that in a matter of weeks he would have feelings for this woman.

Right about now, he wasn't sure how to keep her in his life. But he knew he was going to die trying.

Chapter Twelve

"Is Emery going with us to the rodeo?" Charlie asked on Friday after the vandalism at the garden. They were at the barn getting the horses ready for the rodeo that evening.

Emery hadn't exactly been missing in action, but she'd definitely been scarce all week. She was obviously distancing herself from them. When they left, she wouldn't be with them every day. They would have to get used to being a family, the three of them. He got that.

He didn't like it, though. At all.

He had missed her when he'd taken the girls to Tulsa. The girls had missed her. He'd wanted to give them a chance to see where he lived, to see the town and even his offices. The three of them had talked to a decorator, picked a room that would be theirs and then showed him where to build a chicken coop for their hens and the rooster named Lee. Nan had been unwell, so Emery had remained in Pleasant to care for her.

"I'm not sure," he admitted to her question about Emery. "She might be there."

"Oh," she said quietly. "I hope she'll come to my birthday."

Birthday? Beau wasn't sure what to say.

"You forgot my birthday," she said, a lost look on her face.

He wanted to deny it. But he couldn't. "I'm sorry."

"It's in two weeks, so at least you didn't forget completely."

"Forgive me," he said. "We'll plan a party. We can do whatever you want."

"No, we can't." The words were accompanied by a sheen of moisture in her dark eyes.

She might have said more, except a hint of sound came from the stall where the momma cat kept her kittens and where Cadence liked to hide out.

"Bad kittens, you lost your mittens," Cadence whispered.

Beau and Charlie tiptoed to the edge of the stall and peeked in. Cadence didn't notice them there. She had an orange kitten in her arms, holding it close, one kitten paw in her hand.

"You'll get no dinner," she told the kitten

and then kissed the top of its head. "I love you, kitten."

Charlie shook her head and rushed away, tears streaming down her face. How had something so spectacular caused so much sadness?

"Charlie," he called after her. She didn't stop.

Ethan met him at the door. "What happened?"

"I'm not really sure. Cadence was talking to the kittens and Charlie bolted."

"Talking to kittens? Caddie?"

"Yeah," Beau said. "Which way did she go?"

"She hightailed it around the barn. I tried to stop her."

After searching around the different outbuildings, Beau circled back to the barn. He stood for a moment in the shadowy interior, listening for more than the sound of Ethan talking to Cadence as he loaded saddles in the horse trailer.

As he stood there thinking, praying, he noticed bits of hay falling through the cracks of the wood ceiling, above which was the hayloft.

"Found you," he whispered.

He climbed up the ladder and poked his head through the square opening to the top level of the barn where square bales of hay were stored. In the old days, before round bales, this loft would have been full. Now it was used to store only a few bales for the horses.

He spotted her almost immediately, sitting in a corner on a hay bale.

"Go away," she whispered in a weepy voice that broke his heart.

"I can't." He finished the climb and stood on the floor of the loft. He hadn't been up there in a long time. "We used to make tunnels in the hay sometimes."

"Good for you," she said. "You got to spend your childhood in your home, with your parents."

"Oh, Charlie…" There were no words. He joined her on the hay bale. "I wish I could give you back your parents. I wish that I could make your life exactly what it was and take away all of this heartache. But I can't."

"No duh," she sniffled, and more tears ran down her cheeks. She drew her knees to her chest.

"I'm sorry that I forgot your birthday." He was more sorry than he could say. "We'll plan a big party."

"A big party won't bring them back. A big party won't give our mom back to Caddie, so she can read her stories and kiss her goodnight."

"I know. But you deserve a big party. And you deserve to be a kid, Charlie, a teenager. You've taken great care of Caddie, but you need to be able to just be her sister. I promise, I'm going to do my very best at being a parent to both of you so that you don't have to try and fill that role."

She swallowed and nodded a little before burying her face in her knees, wrapping her arms around her head to complete the cocoon.

"What upset you more, Cadence talking, or me forgetting your birthday?" he asked, trying to draw her out of her shell.

"Both. Mom used to read that story to her and then kiss her on the head. That's what Mom said, 'I love you, kitten.'" And then they both cried and he gathered her up in his arms and held her tight.

"I love you, Charlie Cat."

She sobbed and laughed a little at the same time. "Don't be weird, Beau."

He laugh-cried, too. "I try not to be," he said. And he wished, more than ever, that Emery was there at his side, doing this parenting thing with him.

He noticed that Charlie's phone was next to her and she had a message.

"Someone texted," he said.

She wiped her tears on her sleeve and picked up her phone. "It's Emery."

"Oh, you texted her?"

She nodded. "I told her I needed her."

He totally got that. No matter what, he couldn't convince himself that he just missed her help with the girls. There was more. He just hadn't figured out how much more.

"I'm going to miss her," Charlie said as another tear rolled down her cheek.

"Tulsa isn't that far away. We'll visit," he assured the teen. He didn't mention the part about the job in St. Louis. They'd cross that bridge when they got to it.

"Yeah, sure." She stared at the phone and didn't look any more convinced than he felt. "We'll see her until you date some woman and then there will be another person we have to get used to and someone we might not even like."

"I'm not getting married."

"But someday you might and whoever you're dating, that person will be in our life. We like Emery." The words came out on a sob. "We don't want to leave her."

"We're going to be okay, Charlie." He prayed for the right words, but at the moment, he felt there weren't any. "I know this is difficult."

Understatement of the year.

She gave him a look that proved it. "No, you don't know. You don't have a clue how I feel. You don't understand. I told Caddie to shut her mouth and not act like a baby, to stop crying and stop talking, or she was going to get us killed and…"

He didn't let her push him away. He pulled her close and hugged her tight and he wanted more than ever to take her pain—the way a father would. Over her head, he spotted someone peeking up from the hole in the floor. He released a pent-up breath at the sight of Emery pulling herself up to the floor of the loft.

She made her way slowly to their side and sat down on the hay bale, squeezing in next to Charlie. The dewy look in her gray eyes meant she'd heard at least part of the conversation.

"You are fourteen, Charlie. You're still a child." Emery put an arm around the teen. "You did your very best for yourself and for Cadence. Right now she's downstairs singing to her kitten. Zeb is enjoying the concert from outside the stall, because he's afraid of cats. You kept her safe! She's with those kittens because you were there for her. You are both alive because you made hard decisions that day."

"It hurts so much," Charlie said as she leaned into Emery.

"I know," Emery agreed, still holding the girl tight.

Beau wiped his eyes and wanted more than anything to bring his friends back for the sake of their daughters. That couldn't happen. He was it. He had to step up and be the person they needed.

The woman sitting with him on the bale of hay in the dusty, airless hayloft was the missing piece to this family. He knew it deep down.

When and how they would make this family, those were the unanswered questions.

"We should go," Charlie said after they'd been sitting there for some time.

Emery continued to hold her close, stroking her hair, praying for her to heal, to find joy in life in spite of the pain, the loss she'd suffered. It could happen, Emery knew. She herself had experienced the healing, the unexplained joy in the midst of difficult situations.

She'd experienced God.

A God she really needed right now, in this place. In a musty, dusty hayloft where a girl's heart was breaking from her grief, where a man struggled to find the right words. And Emery left her own heart out of the equation because her heart should have known better. *She* had known better.

"How did you even get up here?" Charlie asked with a sniffle.

"Same way you did," Emery said simply, as if she wasn't worried about how she would get back down. "Is there a slide going down? I could really use a slide."

Charlie laughed at that. "I don't think so, but that would be fun."

They started to get up from the hay bale, wiping off bits and pieces of dried clover, the sweet smell hanging in the air. Beau reached for Emery and she slipped her hand into his, letting him pull her to her feet. As they walked back to the ladder, his arm went around her waist and she leaned on him for support.

It felt natural. It felt safe. It scared the living daylights out of her.

She rarely allowed herself to lean on anyone, not this way. She didn't want to feel weak, to seem incapable.

"Charlie, you go first." Beau continued to keep a hand around Emery's waist. "Be careful."

"I will," she said, then she rushed him, wrapping her arms around him and hugging him tight. "I know you're sorry you have us, but I'm glad my mom and dad picked you."

He closed his eyes.

"I am not sorry," he said. "I love you and Caddie. I know I'm not very good at this parenting business, but I'm glad they picked me, too."

"I'm sorry for being so difficult," she said as she sat on the edge of the floor, her feet dangling. "I'll do better."

"*We* will do better," Beau assured her.

Charlie turned and began the climb back down the ladder.

"Ready?" Beau asked as he sat down on the edge of the exit, taking Emery with him. She eased her way down and then they were sitting side by side, feet dangling over the edge and the ladder there, waiting for them.

"I'll go down first," he told her. "I'll be there to catch you."

"Will you?" She leaned to look over at the ground a good twelve feet down.

"Another smile. I'm going to start rewarding myself for those."

"I do smile even when you're not around, so don't let it go to your head."

"Do you?" he asked, his expression too serious as he looked up at her.

"I do." The words came out softer than she'd intended, with too much longing.

Longing was dangerous. It made her want more than she'd resigned her life to having. A long time ago she'd added a verse to Nan's needlepoint stitching that hung on the dining room wall. Yes, she was more than a conqueror, but she had also learned to be content in the life she had. She'd learned what it meant to not have enough and to sometimes have plenty, but wherever she was at in life, no matter her situation, she'd learned to be happy, to be content. Now? Now she wanted more. Being a part of this journey with Beau and the girls, she found herself truly longing for a family, other than her mother and sisters, to share her life with.

"Come to the rodeo with us?" he asked as he eased his way down the ladder. He was looking up at her, dimples splitting his cheeks as if he knew the direction of her thoughts.

For a moment she held her breath, the old fear coming back, the one that warned her that very soon someone would yank the rug out from under her, and she'd fall flat on her face, embarrassed for having hoped.

She shook her head at him.

"Stop distracting me. I have to concentrate on this."

He'd reached the bottom and now stood on the ground, still looking up. "I'm here," he assured her.

"I know."

She studied the ladder, trying to figure out the best way down. Coming up it hadn't been this difficult. She finally put her good leg down, caught the rung, then turned herself facing in.

"You've got this," Beau encouraged.

She looked down. "I have a confession to make."

"What's that?"

"I'm afraid of heights, and also, I have no feeling in my left foot," she told him. "Please watch and make sure I get my foot on a rung. I really don't want to slide all the way down."

"I won't let you fall."

"Too—" She clamped her mouth closed, shocked at what she'd almost said. *Too late.* She'd already fallen…for Beau.

She made it to the ground and then stood for a moment, getting her bearings. Beau handed her the crutches she'd left leaning against a stall door.

"Thank you," she said as her cheeks heated.

"Thank *you*, for coming over like that, for being here for Charlie."

"No problem," Emery told him. "Beau, I don't mind being here, for you and for the girls."

He rubbed a hand across his eyes. "I'm no good at this, any of this."

"You are," she told him, fighting the urge to put her arms around him.

He blew out a breath. "Caddie was talking to the kitten and repeating what Dana would say after reading her the story about the five little kittens."

"I know." Emery touched his arm, needing to comfort him. "Charlie told me."

She leaned her crutches against the wall and

embraced him. His arms were around her waist. It was a dangerous thing, this hug. It felt too right.

But it was all wrong. She could hold him for a moment. But she couldn't hold him, or the girls, forever. She'd once told Nan that she wasn't the girl whom anyone thought about marrying. She was sweet and pretty Emery, the best friend, the third wheel.

"Hey, are we going to the rodeo or not?"

She and Beau jumped away from each other at the sudden question.

"Oops, sorry," Ethan said, not sounding very sorry.

"Yep, almost ready." Beau waved his brother away. "You're going with us to the rodeo, right?"

She needed to say no. It was the wisest decision. But she knew she was needed this night, to hold Cadence, to encourage Charlie.

She sighed, closing her eyes as she nodded. "Yes, I'll go. In my own car. I've had enough of you driving me around everywhere."

She smiled, for him, and because of him.

"For that smile, I'd take you anywhere you wanted to go."

"Your brother is waiting." She backed away and became aware of a furry presence at her side. "Zeb. I wondered where you'd gotten to."

Fortunately, Charlie spotted them and hurried their way.

"Are you going with us?" Charlie asked, her face aglow, the way a teenager's face should be. "To the rodeo grounds? I'm going to ride True in the barrel racing event."

The teen was practically bouncing, she was so excited. The discussion in the hayloft, the shock of Cadence telling the kitten her story, was all forgotten.

"Yes, I'll go," Emery said.

"Will you ride with us?" Charlie glanced back at the barn. "Oh, I have to go. Uncle Ethan told me to get my own saddle. If I'm really going to ride, I have to take care of my horse and my tack."

Charlie raced off and Emery found herself laughing.

Beau studied her face, his dark eyes warm.

"What?" she asked.

He looked so unbelievably handsome as he swept off his cowboy hat and stepped close to her.

"I really want to kiss you," he said softly, leaning close and making her want the same.

"Why?"

He chuckled. "You're beautiful, kind, adorable…" He leaned in, bringing his face close to hers. "Do I need to go on?"

"No…"

"So… I can't kiss you?" He seemed disappointed.

"You need to stop talking now."

She wrapped her right arm around his waist and he pulled her close, his embrace gentle. His lips touched hers, capturing her heart and soul. Gently he kissed her, his hand warm and strong on her back.

When he kissed her cheek, then her temple, she almost felt a sense of loss.

"Beau," she whispered.

"Shhh, don't. No objections. No 'we shouldn'ts.' We did and I'll never regret it."

"Beau," she tried again.

He kissed her quickly, his mouth stopping her from speaking.

"Emery," he whispered close to her ear. "Shhh."

"The girls," she managed to say.

"Girls?"

"If we don't want to give the girls the wrong idea, I should probably walk away." Someday Beau would marry. The girls would have a woman in their lives again, someone who would love them, care for them.

"The girls," he said, releasing her.

She instantly missed the strength of his arms around her.

"I'm not sure what to say," she told him.

"Let's not say anything," he advised. "I don't want either of us to ruin this by saying something that we'll later regret."

She nodded, agreeing. Together they slowly walked to the door of the barn. Ethan met them, his eyes narrowing as he studied them from beneath his black cowboy hat.

"Are you going to help?" Ethan asked.

"Nah," Beau teased. "I'm the little brother. I'm never helpful and I always get what I want."

Ethan gave him a look. "I might have told you that a time or two, but I'm older and wiser now and I know it isn't true. Get your saddle."

"Fine." Beau winked at Emery as he headed for the tack room.

The teasing between brothers had lightened the mood, but it didn't take away the regret settling in her heart.

The kiss had been everything she'd ever imagined. Sweet, powerful, real. But it only increased the longing she'd felt earlier for a life that wasn't hers to take.

She needed to put distance between herself, Beau and the girls. Sooner rather than later, before any hearts were broken. She knew all too well that she would be the one left behind picking up the shattered remnants of her heart. It was a process she knew all too well. She also knew how she'd feel when they left Pleasant.

Bereft.

Chapter Thirteen

In the end, Beau convinced Emery to drive her car to Nan's and leave it. He picked her up there and they rode together to the rodeo grounds. The girls were in the back seat, Charlie talking the whole way. He was glad, because her chatter kept him from thinking about the woman at his side and their kiss.

The next couple of hours flew by. The event was a local ranch rodeo with youth and adult barrel racing along with other events. Barrel racing was the last event of the night. He stood next to the bleacher where Emery sat holding a very sleepy Cadence.

They didn't talk. All night he'd noticed the shift in her, the way she seemed to be distancing herself. She'd closed down and he could guess why. Maybe the kiss, but he also thought she feared the closeness growing between them.

He got it. He could admit that he was a little bit afraid of what he felt for her. The attraction aside, there was a connection that felt as if it should be forever. A connection she was fighting and he was fighting to hold on to.

At the back of the arena, he could see Ethan with Charlie. They'd both insisted he come out here and watch the event. The two had different reasons. Ethan didn't want him to miss Charlie's first competition. Charlie wanted him to stop making her nervous.

"Sit down," Emery offered, pulling him back to the present.

Man, she was beautiful, poised and she was making room for him. Next to her, not in her life.

She said something to Zeb and the dog switched sides, sitting obediently on her right side, giving him the space on the left.

"I think I'm too nervous," he admitted. But he sat down anyway.

"She'll do great."

"I know," he said absently. "It's True's first time, too. That means two beginners in the arena together. What if the horse gets spooked, or what if…?"

"And you thought you couldn't parent. Listen to you, being all dad-ish." She patted his arm in a friendly way that didn't give an opening for him to take her hand in his.

"Yeah, this parenting thing is like wearing boots that are too tight."

"Just watch," she said. The command startled him and he jumped a little, but he did watch.

True and Charlie were in the opening, about to make their run. He watched as the teenager got her seat, leaning just a little, holding the reins just the way he'd taught her. He couldn't have been any prouder. She came out like a champ, the little filly hanging right with her.

He cheered her on, shouting from the sideline as she rounded the third barrel and headed home. The stands, filled with local citizens who knew Charlie and had known her parents, were on their feet, cheering with him. It hit him in the heart, the love the community was pouring out on Garret and Dana's daughter.

In the end, she came in third, but the glow on her face made her the true winner. After the ribbons and trophies were awarded, they returned to the horse trailer to unsaddle and brush down their animals. Beau picked Cadence up, setting her on the tailgate of his pickup truck. Emery followed. Cadence climbed onto her lap, thumb in her mouth. She was sleepy.

He was sleepy, too. Sometimes he managed

to forget about being hospitalized. Nights like tonight, when it hit him like a semitruck, he remembered.

"You okay?" Ethan asked as they were loading tack.

Beau pushed his hat back, taking a moment to breathe and welcome the breeze and cooler night air. "I'm good. Tired."

"You're not looking so great," his brother said as he loaded the last saddle.

"Stop big brothering. We need to load horses and get the girls home."

"Charlie has company," Ethan said quietly. "She sometimes seems to be trying to push Quinn away, but Quinn is relentless."

Beau looked over to Charlie. She had tied True and was brushing the mare down, every now and then slipping her a piece of carrot from the stash she kept in her pockets.

Quinn, Avery and Grayson Stone's daughter, appeared at her side, a wide grin on her face. "You were great, Charlie. Congratulations."

Charlie looked startled but a little bit pleased. "You won first. Congratulations."

Quinn blushed. "Thank you."

The two girls had a quiet conversation that ended with hugs and Quinn telling Charlie that they would get together soon. Maybe they could have a sleepover. Sleepovers! Beau hadn't thought about that. Young girls invading his home.

He was going to need help.

Beau couldn't stop his gaze from straying to Emery. There she sat, on the tailgate with Cadence in her arms and Zeb sprawled out in the bed of the truck. She became aware of him staring and lifted her head, startling him with the depth of emotion in her expression. Everything about her moved him.

"I'll meet you back at the house," Ethan said as he rounded the back of the trailer, pulling his keys from his pocket. He stopped, shook his head and groaned. "You're going to have to control that."

"What?" Beau jerked his attention away from Emery. Charlie appeared at his side, a knowing look on her face. He wanted to ignore both of them.

"I haven't seen that look on your face since Lori Pruett shared her peanut butter and jelly with you in fifth grade," Ethan said with a wry chuckle.

Beau rolled his eyes. "Time to go. Charlie, you ready?"

"Nope, I'm riding with Uncle Ethan. I'll help him get the horses unloaded and saddles put away."

"Okay, then." He swept a look around the arena. "This was fun, but I'll be sore tomorrow."

"You're getting soft with all that big-city life," Ethan said as he headed for the driver's side of his truck.

"Right."

"I'll be there as soon as I drop Emery at Nan's."

They loaded up in his truck, buckling a sleepy Cadence in the back. Refusing his help, Emery grabbed the handle on the inside of the truck and pulled herself up. "See, I can do it."

"I think you can do anything you set your mind to."

She gave him a long look, then shook her head. "Don't."

He didn't ask for clarification, didn't say anything further. He closed the door and headed for the driver's side, waving to a couple of neighbors nearby who were still loading up. Tucker Church had brought the steers for several events. He and Grayson were loading up their livestock trailers.

Even after all of these years, Pleasant still felt like home. He used to think it was the last place he wanted to be.

"Why are you frowning?" Emery asked as they pulled onto the main road.

"I never expected to want to be here again," he admitted.

"Why?" she asked. "I mean, I know the reasons I wanted to escape Pleasant. What are yours?"

"I think I needed to go somewhere and be my own person. I wanted city life, something other than raising cattle and planting crops. I thought I was escaping." He gave a dry laugh. "Being back home, I realize I've missed it. But I don't know if missing it means I want to be back here on a permanent basis. I'm also not sure if running the dealerships is where I'm supposed to be or if it's just temporary until my dad can get back to doing what he loves."

She gave him a thoughtful look.

"Sorry, that was more than I planned on saying," he said.

"You don't have to apologize," she said. "What do you want to do with your life, Mr. Wilde?"

He grinned at that. "I can't give away all my secrets," he told her.

"I think that whatever it is, you shouldn't put it off."

She grew silent as they turned onto the county road that ran along the riverbanks. He glanced her way and saw that she was studying the passing scenery, her hands clasped tightly in her lap.

"Is something wrong?" he asked. Maybe she

was thinking about the kiss, about the past or about saying goodbye.

She shook her head, but it wasn't an answer.

Her worried expression had to be about more than their coming goodbyes. He had a feeling the past had crept in and she was fighting memories. Only, he didn't know what had caused her to remember and he didn't know how to make it better. Or if he could.

The cold seeped into Emery, chilling her. She pushed the vents down so the air-conditioning wouldn't blow against her. It didn't help. The cold came from deep inside, where memories were buried.

"Emery?" Beau's voice drew her back to the present.

"Yes?"

"Are you okay? You're pale." He reached for her hand. "And cold."

She stared out the window. The fog that hovered over the river moved slowly, encroaching on the banks, covering the trees. "I grew up down here. I hardly ever take this road because I don't enjoy driving past that house."

"I'm sorry, I didn't think about that."

She managed to nod and not cry. "I wouldn't expect you to."

"No one should ever go through what you went through."

"No, they shouldn't." She drew in a breath, tried to gather some strength. "I've gone through a lot of therapy to be able to say that I forgive my parents. I forgive my mother for leaving me, and my father for abusing me, emotionally and physically."

His hand still held hers, warming her, giving her someone solid and caring to hold on to.

"I really don't like myself very much right now," he said.

"I like you fine as an adult. Also, you're forgiven. I think I needed this, getting to know you, to stop thinking of you as that boy and to finally forgive you."

His hand released hers. He downshifted and turned onto the road to Nan's. "I'd like to think this time together is about more than forgiveness."

He sounded hurt. She didn't want to hurt him. She didn't want to give him her heart, either. But she realized that might have already happened. She'd protected herself for so many years that it felt uncomfortable to let someone in, to take chances.

She did believe that she was more than a conqueror, but at the moment, her armor was slipping and fear had edged in. The kiss had frightened her. The idea of him leaving shook her to the core.

"Emery?" He gave her a puzzled look as they pulled up to Nan's, the security light casting his features in a pale light.

"This is where we say goodbye." Her voice trembled as she said the words. Her hand was on the door, ready to escape. She reached for her crutches and whispered to Zeb. She wanted to run, because this way lay heartache, and in Nan's house there was safety.

She was a twenty-nine-year-old coward.

"Goodbye sounds pretty final to me."

"Some friendships are for a season, Beau. Maybe that's why I was here, in this place at this time. This was our season of forgiving. Our season of healing. We're at a place where we discover the next season, the next path. I know we'll still see each other, but it's time to start the separation process, for your sake and for the girls'. And the longer I stay in the mix, the harder it will be for us all to go our separate ways. The girls are relying on us to make it easy for them."

She called herself a coward. But she wasn't thinking only of Beau and the girls. She was thinking of her own heart and how it would feel to let them go. If she made it about them, it might hurt a little less.

"I can't imagine doing this without you," he admitted. "I don't know what I would have done if you hadn't agreed to help."

She opened the truck door. When he started to move, to get out and help, she stopped him with a shake of her head. "I can do this. And you, you're going to be just fine."

"Emery, I don't want to lose you. I think there could be something wonderful here between us and I want to figure that out."

"This isn't real," she told him. "It's based on the situation we found ourselves in, helping the girls. In time you'll realize that and thank me for knowing when to walk away."

"Is that your professional opinion? If so, I disagree."

She shook her head. "Once you get back to your real life, to your home, your job and the people you normally surround yourself with, you'll realize I'm right. This was a hugely emotional time for you, for the girls and even for me. Emotions get confused in situations like this."

"I thought you knew me better than that," he said. "I'll go, but I want to make it very clear that what I feel for you is real."

She had hoped he would stay in his truck, making this easier for both of them. He didn't. Of course he got out. Of course he didn't give her space. She should have walked away. Instead, she stood there frozen to the ground, the full moon shining down on them.

"Emery, you are a beautiful, educated, kind human being who knows a lot about helping people through difficult times. But you don't know the first thing about relationships. I'm no expert, either, but I do know that this is special and not something to walk away from."

He kissed her and she couldn't help but kiss him back. She agreed that they did share something. She also knew that they were on the road to heartbreak. It was a given, a definite, that he'd break her heart.

Separating herself from him, she touched his cheek and tried to memorize how he looked standing there in front of her, how it felt when he touched her as if she was precious to him.

"I'm physically and emotionally broken, Beau. I'm working on it, but that's something I don't want to burden anyone with. And maybe it's the coward's way out, but if I walk away now, you can't hurt me."

She walked away, Zeb at her side. For the first time ever, her dog gave her a look that seemed to ask if she'd lost her mind.

Emery made it to the porch somehow, holding back tears and telling herself she'd done the right thing. She sat on the porch swing. Zeb hopped up next to her, setting the swing in motion. She gestured with her hand, and he stretched out, his front paws and head on her lap. The truck circled the drive and left.

She prayed for Beau and the girls. That seemed the easiest way to let them go. Yes, she would see them from time to time, but letting go was a process. She'd loved having them in her life.

She closed her eyes, letting the sounds and smells of the country night lull her into a peaceful place as she prayed. The screen door squeaked on its hinges. She opened her eyes and smiled at Avery as she stepped outside. Zeb slid off the swing, greeting her with a nose to her hand, an invitation to pet him.

Avery gave the dog's ears some attention, then sat next to Emery. People used to believe the two of them were biological sisters because of their similar heights and face shapes. But Avery had blond hair, Emery's was dark. They shared no DNA, but they did share a woman who had given them both hope, faith, healing and self-worth. The latter sometimes seemed the hardest to hold on to.

"How was the rodeo?" Avery asked as she gave the swing a little push.

"Good. Quinn did great, and so did Charlie. I wish you could have been there."

"Not with a sickly baby. This damp night air is the last thing she needs with her croupy cough. Anyway, I felt better staying here with Nan. She doesn't enjoy being here alone at night." Avery stopped the swing. "Which leads me to the topic of your job opportunity. Nan knows. She heard Louis's wife telling someone about it. She thinks you're going to turn it down because of her and she doesn't want that."

Emery sighed. "I didn't want her to know."

Avery gave the swing a little push, but she kept her attention focused. "Go talk to the people at this facility and see if it's where you're supposed to be. At least then you'll know and you won't always wonder what if."

"I'll think about it." She exhaled loudly at the look Avery gave her. "You know, you're not that much older than me and yet you're playing the big sister card right now."

They were both silent for several minutes.

"Nan is trying to make a plan for the future. She knows it's only a matter of time before she can no longer take care of this place. She put the farm in trust several years back. And she wants to find the right person to take over the boat shop. She would like it to be one of us, her girls."

Emery brushed a hand over her face. "This isn't how Nan's story ends."

"I know this is hard, but we can't ignore it."

"No, we can't." She closed her eyes and tried to regain the calm she'd felt earlier. "This really stinks," Emery whispered as she reached to pet Zeb. Her heart ached at the thought of facing the future.

"Yeah, it does, but we'll all get through it together." After a few minutes of silence, Avery asked, "So, why are you sitting out here on the porch alone? I peeked out the window and it looked as if you and Beau were arguing. Did he say something to upset you?"

She felt a rush of warmth for the woman the courts had made her sister. "No, we didn't argue. I was telling him goodbye. The girls have been through a lot. I don't want them to think that we're a family, the four of us. I want them to be able to move to Tulsa and settle into their new lives."

"Without you?" Avery shook her head, clearly confused. "Why can't you be in their lives?"

"Because they need to move on. I'm sure Beau will date. He might even get married. If I'm in the mix, that's confusing."

"I might be wrong, but it seemed like there might be something between the two of you."

"Yeah, heartache and trouble," she quipped.

"Just because he hurt you as a teenager doesn't mean he will hurt you now."

"I know, but I also don't want to be—" she hesitated to say it "—the woman a man comes to regret. The woman he has to slow down and wait for. The woman who can't have children. I…"

"Oh, honey, why do you do this to yourself? You deserve to love and be loved. Trust a man to love you enough that he will even love the things that you see as weaknesses in yourself. When you are loved and allow yourself to be loved, it heals things."

"I'm fine. I just…" She leaned to kiss the top of Zeb's head. "I've had a lifetime of hurt and I don't want to take chances. I also don't want to go into a relationship and then tell a man that I probably can't have a baby."

"Get checked out, Emmy. Go to the doctor and get another opinion. Yes, you had an infection. Your father and his worthless friends hurt you, but wounds heal, both physical and emotional. You're healing, so why not see if your body has healed as well?"

"I have one fallopian tube and it's scarred." She closed her eyes to the tears that stung and tried to fall. Her throat tightened with the effort to remain calm.

"Modern medicine is amazing and there are

plenty of ways of helping women who want to have children."

"I know." She wiped at a tear that escaped. "But it's a big maybe and that's a lot for a man to deal with. Maybe I can have babies. Maybe I won't cringe every time someone hugs me or sneaks up behind me in the kitchen."

"Do you cringe when Beau hugs you?"

"No, I don't."

"You could tell him the truth. All of it."

"That's a lot for someone to deal with. *Please like me, because I had a very disturbing childhood. I've gone to a lot of therapy and I know Jesus, but here it is, the story of my childhood.* The man stays because he feels sorry for you. But then later he feels trapped."

"You think about this way too much and far too deeply," Avery accused.

"Maybe I do," she agreed.

"A doctor gave you the worst-case scenario. It's time for you to learn the best-case scenario. It's time for you to trust that God has a plan, because you are His. Stop telling yourself what you think and feel, and ask God what He thinks."

"I'll think about it," Emery said. "But I don't think it changes anything. Beau isn't the one for me."

It was much easier to be the one who said

goodbye than the one who walked away brokenhearted.

It was a lesson she'd learned early and one she had a difficult time letting go of.

Chapter Fourteen

It seemed hard to believe that it could be mid-June already. They'd been out of school for two weeks. Emery wanted the summer to go slower. She wanted more time to enjoy Nan and more time to think about the job offer at the residential facility. It would be a four-hour drive from Pleasant. Two years ago, she wouldn't have given it a second thought. Now the decision required lots of thoughts and a lot of prayer.

As Emery walked across the lawn with Zeb, she noticed the drying grass, a sign they needed rain. June should have been a rainy month, not a hot and dry month. The community garden would need to be watered tomorrow when she met with the students. She'd been trying to water it at least every other day. Jarod and Lila both lived in town, so they took turns going over there and watering. They had lettuce coming in, cherry tomatoes and zucchini that were getting ripe.

She continued to let her thoughts roam, because that kept her from thinking about Beau, Charlie and Cadence. She wouldn't lie to herself that the sadness she felt was only about the girls. She missed him.

It was a difficult place to find herself, missing the person who just a dozen years ago she'd been all too happy to never see again. A month ago, when he'd arrived to take custody of the girls, she'd been angry for herself, frightened for them and convinced he couldn't possibly have changed.

Now she missed him. She paused in her walk to the boat shop, adjusted her crutches and took a breath. Sometimes a person needed to do that, just breathe. Pray. Find peace in a decision that hadn't been easy. Find peace in decisions yet to be made.

She could hear Nan's sander and gospel music so loud that it could probably be heard a block away coming from the boat shop. Nan always wanted to be able to hear the music over the power tools and even through the headphones she wore to protect her hearing.

As Emery entered the shop, Nan looked up and gave a quick wave. Zeb wiggled, his brown eyes gazing up at Emery, pleading.

"Go," she told him. He made a beeline for Nan and the dog treats she kept for him.

Nan put her sander down, then pulled off the noise-reducing headphones and goggles that she wore. She welcomed Zeb, rubbing his ears and face the way he loved. She whispered to him and he sat, although not patiently. He knew the dog biscuits were in the cabinet and he glanced that way, giving Nan small barks of encouragement.

Lately it seemed as if Nan needed Zeb more than Emery. She'd brought him home two years ago and in those two years she realized his role had changed. He continued to be her service dog, her companion, but he willingly shared his affection with anyone in need.

"What are you up to this morning?" Nan asked her as she doled out the treats.

"I'm going to town."

"You're a good boy, Zeb." Nan gave him a third treat.

"You spoil him," Emery said as she took a seat across from Nan. She ran a hand down the sanded sides of the johnboat. It had three bench seats, cup holders, and a live well for a fisherman to hold his catch.

"What do you think?" Nan asked as she sat down on her work stool.

"It's very nice. Is it sold?"

"Yes, to a very nice man. He's the big outdoor store guy. For the life of me, I can't think of his name. We talked on the phone. He called me personally because he didn't want anyone else to handle this. It's a gift."

"He obviously wants the best."

"You seem down," Nan observed. "Is this about the job, or about the girls?"

She wished Nan hadn't found out about the job offer.

"The job isn't for me," Emery answered, without really giving an answer.

"It's an amazing opportunity," Nan said with a steely tone. "Do not let me or my silly brain keep you from doing what you want to do. If you feel this is the right position for you, then you should take it. Everything else will work itself out."

"Nan, I'm where I want to be right now." Because there were seasons in life, and in this season, she needed to be here, near Nan. And Nan needed her close.

"Emery, I want you to consider taking the job. I know that I'm forgetful, but I haven't forgotten your dreams, or the way you always talked about someday helping children. I know you love your job at the school, but the other job is what you've been training for."

Emery couldn't bring herself to look at Nan, because she spoke the truth.

"Could the problem be that you miss Beau and the girls? You haven't been spending a lot of time with them." Nan's voice was sweetly gentle, the voice of a mother who knew her child.

They'd discussed her decision to distance herself from Beau and the girls. But Nan had forgotten, so Emery repeated the explanation, instead of reminding Nan of the conversation that had taken place mere days ago.

"They'll be leaving at the end of the month and I thought it would be better for the girls if they adjusted to the fact that I wouldn't be around every day." She missed them more than she ever dreamed she would. Every day since last Friday she'd thought of them.

Even though she'd seen them at church, it hadn't been the same as spending time with them at the Rocking W or even at school. She reminded herself that this was what distancing meant. It meant time and space between them.

If only she could distance her thoughts from them.

When she'd driven up to the residential facility to take a tour and talk to the director, she'd thought about Beau and what he'd think about the facility and the job offer. She had six months to go on her doctorate. When she finished, she'd be overqualified for her current job and she feared they would let her go out of concern that she would want more money. A small school in Pleasant didn't have deep pockets.

"Are you sure this is the right way to handle the situation? It seems so heartbreaking for the girls to lose someone else they love."

"They're leaving and I might possibly be leaving, too. If I take this job, I'll be almost six hours away from them." She shrugged because she didn't know the right answer. She wasn't sure she knew what direction to go.

Nan sat there for a moment holding her empty coffee cup. "Are you doing this for the girls or to protect your own heart?"

"I'm doing this because it's the best thing for everyone."

Nan set her coffee cup on the table and picked up a small square of sandpaper. "What if Beau and those girls are your path in life, Emery? What if you're avoiding the real plan for your future?"

She nearly laughed. "You're not very subtle."

Nan grinned, and that warmed Emery's heart. Nan had a smile that made everything okay. "Sweet girl, I've never tried to be subtle. These days, I don't have time for subtle."

"I love you," Emery said, her voice tightening.

"I love you more," Nan returned. "I just want you to be happy."

"I know." This crushed her. It made her heart feel hollow and clogged her throat. Zeb had finished his treat and came to rest his furry chin on her knee.

"Oh, tomorrow," Nan said as if everything was fine, as if they hadn't been talking about something that would devastate them all.

"What about tomorrow?" Emery's throat remained tight.

Nan blew out a breath. "Well, I…" She looked to heaven and then smiled. "Oh, yes, someone is coming here to talk to me about the boats."

"To buy a boat?"

Nan shook her head. "Nope, to buy the boat shop."

Nan went to work, smoothing out the inside of the cup holder, as if she hadn't just dropped a bombshell into the conversation.

"But, Nan, these are your boats. No one else can make your boats."

"Emery, we both know that I'm not going to be able to do this much longer. You're not going to make boats because you'll soon be Dr. Emery Guthrie, PhD. Avery is a nurse. Clara is helping Tucker turn the river into a float trip and camping gold mine."

"I just think one of us could take over,"

Emery continued, trying to think of one of her foster sisters, one of Nan's girls, who might take over the making of her boats.

"I'm selling it, Emery. Not the farm, just the shop."

"To someone local?"

Nan made a puzzled face, shook her head and went back to work. Emery blew her a kiss and left. She had work to do. She was also considering taking a short float later. Or maybe she'd take a kayak. A little time on the slow-moving James River would help her get her thoughts together.

Maybe if she took a few hours, just herself and Zeb on the water, she could find some peace about the decision she seemed on the verge of making. A decision that would take her far from Pleasant, from Nan and also from the memories of Beau Wilde, memories that were no longer about a bully, but a man who made her feel more than she'd ever expected.

"Where have you been?" Ethan asked from underneath the tractor.

"Taking care of business." Which meant "none of your business." Beau doubted his brother would let it go, but he didn't have any intentions of talking. Not yet.

The only person he needed to talk to was his

father. They'd talked for a good long hour the night before. It had been an honest conversation, long overdue.

"Thanks for watching the girls," he added. At the moment, they were messing with the pony Ethan had bought for Cadence. It seemed the child was growing more comfortable with her four-legged friend. She stood next to him, Charlie close at hand, running a brush down his neck while he grabbed a bit of grain from a bucket on the ground in front of him.

"No problem. Little dude kept an eye on them."

"The horse."

"You got it. Never a better babysitter, or so Dad used to tell Mom."

"I remember." Beau laughed a little at the memories that he and Ethan shared. They'd been wild, the two of them. They were lucky they hadn't broken more than the occasional arm.

Beau squatted so he could see what his brother was up to under the big green-and-yellow machine. "What are you doing?"

"If I knew, we'd both be surprised." Ethan banged on something. "But I don't know. I just know that it isn't driving the way it should."

"Want me to take a look?"

Ethan eased his way out from underneath the

tractor. "Nah, not today. I do need to get it fixed so I can cut some hay this week, before it all dries up. Man, we need rain."

"Yeah, we do," Beau agreed. "You'd probably be better off sending it to Lynn. He'll fix it and save you the money of having to buy a new one."

"Yeah, I'll have to take it to him."

From where they sat, they could see Charlie and Cadence in the arena. Cadence now sat on the pony and Charlie led her around, staying close to her side. She was almost fifteen. He noticed she smiled more than she had a month ago. She even laughed on occasion. He had a good dose of fear concerning the coming years. Raising two girls hadn't been part of his plan, but here they were and he knew they'd survive it. With plenty of mistakes thrown in along the way.

He wondered when he would get past the need to call Emery and ask her opinion or tell her something funny or sad that had happened.

"Will she ever really talk, do you think?" Ethan asked, a welcome interruption to thoughts that would probably take him down a well he couldn't climb out of. Missing Emery.

"I hope so. A word here or there is a good sign and we know she talks to her animals. Even that rooster. She carries that thing around like it's the best pet ever."

"I'm glad she likes him. He chased me all the way across the yard the other day."

"I wish I could have seen that. We'd be Instatok famous."

"That isn't a thing," Ethan told him.

They sat for a minute, watching as Charlie instructed Cadence on proper reining.

"I hope she'll be okay in time. She misses Emery." Beau stood back up.

"Yeah, about that…"

"Don't."

"I have to," Ethan said as he got up, brushing off his jeans. "Why are you letting her disappear from your lives? Especially when you all seem pretty sullen about it."

"I'm not sullen," Beau retorted as he walked toward the arena to watch the girls. Ethan followed.

"In case I haven't said it, you're doing a good thing here, raising those two girls."

"But am I doing the right thing? I've been thinking about the fact that Garret and Dana added Nan to the will. Just in case I couldn't, Nan would raise the girls. Maybe they would be better off with her?"

For a long few minutes they stood at the fence of the arena, watching the girls. Charlie said something. Cadence giggled. The pony trotted. It was a jarring gait on the short-legged beast and Cadence bounced in the saddle, causing Charlie to reach and steady her.

"That's a puzzle, isn't it?" Ethan said.

"Yeah, one of many." Beau kept his attention on the girls. "What if they'd be better with Nan and Emery?"

"Did Garret and Dana trust you with their children?" Ethan asked, his tone hard.

"Yeah, they did, but they also didn't plan on something like this happening. Who would ever think…" He shook his head, wishing he didn't feel like crying all over again.

"No, they didn't think this would happen, either, but they did plan for it, just in case. They trusted you to raise their girls."

"Right, I know." He drew in a breath and let it out slowly. "This is a game changer. A life changer."

"Yeah, it is." Ethan leaned on the fence, his arms draped over the top rail. "Maybe you and Emery ought to raise those girls together."

"I think that's out of the equation."

"For who?" Ethan asked. "For you or for God? Fortunately, God has more game than you have."

"Maybe you ought to get married and stop acting like a spinster matchmaker. For crying out loud, you're annoying."

"Whoa, that got under your skin. I don't think I've seen that in a while. Let me tell you something, little brother. A month ago, I thought you should stay away from her. I didn't want to see her hurt. Now, maybe I've changed my mind."

Beau rolled his eyes. "We need to find you a wife."

"I'll pass." Ethan nodded toward the girls. Charlie had climbed on behind Cadence and they were riding the pony together around the arena. "That's some happiness. Maybe you'll catch it from them. You seem to have a lot on your mind."

"I do," Beau admitted.

"Want to talk?"

He shook his head. The girls were within hearing range. "We can sit down and talk tonight. After they go to bed."

Charlie led Cadence to the fence. "Are the two of you done being all serious?"

"Who said we were serious?" Ethan asked. "I am never serious."

"This one is." She pointed at Beau. "Lately he's been seriously cranky."

"Mmm-hmm," Ethan said with an arch of a brow.

"Anyway, I just wanted to ask about my birthday party this Sunday. I invited Quinn, of course. Plus, Tucker said his niece Shay would like to come. She seems nice. Who else can we invite?" She tapped her chin as if thinking, but Beau knew she already had a list.

"Just tell me," Beau prompted.

"Have you invited Emery and Nan?" She put a hand on Cadence's leg. "Cadence wants Emery to be there. So do I. We miss her."

"Do you really?" he asked.

Her eyes sparkled with restrained mirth. She was having fun at his expense.

"I haven't invited Emery and Nan. What's the plan for this party of yours? I have the pizza, cake and ice cream ordered. I might get you a gift if you're good."

"Can we do an evening trail ride, like before it gets dark?"

"I think we could. I'll let Tucker and Grayson know to bring horses."

She beamed with happiness. "Thank you." And then she got around to it. "Don't forget to invite Emery."

"Of course not," he said.

Ethan chuckled. "How could you ever forget Emery."

It might have been a big joke to his brother, but he'd never felt more serious. He'd fallen hard for a woman who wanted nothing to do with him. A woman who made him willing to change his life. A woman who, as far as he knew, was probably going to pack up and get as far away from him as possible.

He'd never chased after a woman. But Emery made him rethink that rule, even though he knew he was the last person she wanted in her life.

He hoped to change her mind. Somehow.

Chapter Fifteen

The community garden was thriving. They'd passed the halfway point in June and they were literally starting to see the fruits of their labor. They had ripe cherry tomatoes, zucchini and cucumbers, and the first snap peas had emerged. On this Saturday morning, a few students had gathered. They were tending plants, talking and smiling as they worked. Every now and then Charlie would shoot a look her way, half questioning, half hurt.

"Can we, I mean you, take Nan a few of these green tomatoes?" Charlie asked as she examined the tomato plants. "Last Sunday at church she said she had a hankering for fried green tomatoes."

"If you want to pick a couple, I'll take them home to her."

Jarod walked over to her. "I have about a half

dozen zucchini, Miz Emery. Pastor Matthews said we might leave them in the church foyer. People will grab them as they come through. The cucumbers, too."

"I like that idea," Emery agreed as she pushed herself up from the bench she'd been resting on. "I'll get a basket to put them in."

Zeb left the garden, careful to not step on the plants, and came to sit next to her. She rubbed his ears and he leaned into her. Zeb would miss the kids and the garden.

"Can I take some peas?" Mila asked. She was new to the group and to living in Pleasant. She'd recently been placed in a local foster home.

"Of course you can take some peas," Emery told the girl. "You all take what your family will use. That's the only hard-and-fast rule we have is…"

"Don't take more than you'll use," Jarod said. "Or share."

"My foster mom loves snap peas," Mila said softly, as was her habit. She seemed shy, almost afraid of her own shadow. Emery didn't know her story, but she could guess.

"Then you take whatever you think she could use." Emery slipped an arm around the teenager's shoulders and gave her a quick side hug. Zeb joined them, pushing his nose into the girl's hand. Mila smiled down at the dog, then gave him a loving pat.

"He's a nice dog," Mila said. "We had…" Her voice trailed off.

"Did you have pets before? A dog?"

She nodded, tears filling her eyes as she quickly looked away. "I know it seems silly, but I miss my parents. I miss home."

"I know you do," Emery told her.

"I've made new friends here and they're all nice. My foster family is really nice. Everyone wants to know if I'm happy to be out of my old home." She laughed a little, but the gesture was empty of humor. "They don't understand what it's like to have police show up at your house, to be told you should hug your mom goodbye because you're leaving with strangers. My little sister was so afraid."

"I know," Emery said. "I know. I'm always here if you need to talk."

"Yeah, but talking to the school counselor is what got me in foster care to begin with."

"She didn't mean to hurt you. She was only doing her job."

"I know," Mila said. "I get it. I know that our home was messed up. It's fine. I'm fine."

"It's okay to be *not fine*," Emery told the girl. "You can be fine when you're ready to be fine. Until then, you can be hurt, sad, angry, whatever you need to be as long as you're honest and letting people help."

"Thank you." The girl gave Emery a quick hug. "Jamie, my foster mom, is here. I have to go."

"Yes, you do. Have a good week," Emery told the girl as she hurried off. She turned to the remaining kids. "Before you leave, bag up whatever you want to take. Leave what you don't want in the basket on the table."

The kids all did as she asked, then waved goodbye and ran to their parents' cars. All but Charlie. She waited, standing awkwardly while Emery cleaned up.

"What's up?" Emery asked.

"I thought maybe you'd forgotten my birthday. It's tomorrow."

"Oh!" Emery had forgotten.

"You're invited to the party," Charlie continued glancing toward the parking lot and the truck that was pulling in. "I know you and Beau aren't really talking, but I'd like for you to come."

Emery sat down next to her. "Charlie, I'm not mad at Beau. I'm also not upset with you or Cadence, just in case that thought had crossed your mind."

"Then why don't you ever come over anymore?"

"I was out of town for a few days. Also, I felt like the three of you needed a chance to be a family without my interference."

"Yeah, sure." Charlie fiddled with Zeb's leash. "I miss Zeb, too."

"I'll bring Zeb."

"We're going on a trail ride." Charlie grinned, her earlier gloom melting away.

"That sounds like fun, although Zeb and I usually don't ride horses." Emery forced a smile. "You should go. Beau's waiting."

"It isn't Beau, it's Ethan. Beau had a meeting. He bought a family car." Charlie made a face, then she gave Emery a quick hug goodbye before running to climb in Ethan's truck.

As Emery sat there, surveying the garden, pleased with the outcome, she tried not to dwell on the fact that Beau had willingly accepted her ruling that they distance themselves. She tried not to think about the kisses, the moments, the times they'd shared that had seemed so special. Her heart ached with the loss of the man and those two precious girls.

Her brain told her she'd been silly to ever think there was something between herself and Beau, something worth pursuing further. He'd always been way out of her league.

It didn't matter. Emery was giving serious consideration to the job at the residential facility. Maybe a fresh start was exactly what she needed.

"Let's go home, Zeb." She gave the garden a last look, prayed for the students, prayed no one would harm their work. She made the slow trek to the parking lot.

A truck, battered and sounding as if it might be on its last journey, pulled in and circled the gravel. She tensed, wondering if they saw her. Could this be the person who had caused the damage? Would they seriously show up in broad daylight?

Zeb remained at her side as she picked up her pace. She got to her car, unlocking the door as she did. The truck stopped. She reached for the door as the man jumped out of the driver's side and rounded his truck.

"Not so fast," he growled. He was a bear of a man with wild straw-colored hair.

"Excuse me?" she said nonchalantly, as if she wasn't shaking. When she looked at him a second time, she didn't see his face. She saw her father.

But it wasn't her father. She knew that. Panic tightened in her chest anyway. She took a breath, needing air. Zeb gave a low growl and pushed against her side, making her thankful for his presence.

"You're that school counselor that likes to get

in other people's business. Got the state snooping around my life because of you."

"If you want to talk, we can sit down and discuss this, Mr….?"

"Little. That name ring a bell, Bible thumper?"

"Mr. Little, is there something I can help you with?"

She glanced past him and saw Alex in the passenger seat, his face bruised, his eyes fearful.

"You sent the police to our house," he accused.

"No, I didn't."

He crowed at that, his eyes sparkling with humor and rage. "I see you have a problem with lying. My boy told me you lied about us."

"I didn't lie. And I didn't send the police. I'm going to leave now."

"Dad, leave her alone." Alex jumped out of the truck. His face was so badly beaten that Emery's stomach rolled.

"I'm not going to have her spreading lies about us." Oscar grabbed her by the arm. "And I'm sure not putting up with her holier-than-thou attitude."

"How do you plan on stopping me?" she asked Oscar, proud that her voice sounded strong and didn't shake the way her legs were.

"I'll figure it out." He came at her. Zeb growled.

The dog distracted him for just a moment, giving Emery a break. She punched the towering giant in the throat and tried to move away, praying someone would drive by and see.

Oscar fell back only a foot or so, but he kept his grip on Emery's arm, yanking her off balance. Zeb sank his teeth into the man's leg, causing Oscar to scream at the dog and kick him hard in the side. Zeb yelped as he landed on the ground. From the corner of her eye, Emery saw Alex take off running.

"Get back here, boy!" Oscar pushed Emery against the car. She tried to move away from him, but he swung around, connecting his fist with her head, then pushing her to the ground.

Emery landed hard on her back, knocking the air from her lungs. She remained where she landed, trying to catch her breath. Zeb had regained his feet and he moved to her side.

"Now what am I supposed to do with you?"

"Leave while you can," she said, gasping for air.

"Shut up."

She clamped her mouth shut, because her head seemed to be spinning and the sun seemed to be fading. She wanted to move, to get away, but if she did, she might vomit.

In the distance, she heard the screech of car tires braking.

"Great, now look what you've done."

"I haven't done anything," she whispered through clenched teeth.

"Shut up," he yelled, his face turning red as he rushed at her.

Her life didn't flash before her eyes. But she did think about Nan, about Beau and the girls. All of those thoughts raced through her mind as Oscar Little grabbed her hair and shoved her head into the side of her car.

Beau rushed through the halls of the Ozarks Community Hospital, a twenty-minute drive from Pleasant. The phone call had come in as he finished up a meeting. He'd called Ethan immediately, explaining he'd be home late because Emery had been taken to the hospital. Beaten by Alex Little's father.

He'd gotten a call from Nan, telling him what had happened, but he didn't know all the details.

He found Nan in the waiting room, sitting with Avery, Clara and their families.

"What happened?" he asked as he stood there in the center of the room, fear for a woman who was not his coursing through him. He wanted to hit something, or someone, and he'd never been a violent person.

"Sit down," Tucker said, nodding toward a

vacant chair. "I can't talk when someone towers over me like that."

"What happened!" Beau repeated as he sat down. Zeb whimpered and came to his side. He put a hand under the dog's furry chin and gave him a good look. "You okay, bud?"

Zeb pushed at his hand, needing comfort.

"Oscar Little went to the church after everyone left and he beat her pretty badly," Avery told him. "She's going to be okay. She's badly bruised and sore."

"How did she get here?" he asked, needing to know. He hadn't been there. If he hadn't been in a meeting, he would have been there to get the girls. Maybe he could have stopped this from happening.

He brushed a hand over his face, wanting to undo everything that had happened. At this point, he even wanted to undo his feelings for her, because if he hadn't started falling for her, feeling as if he had a chance, she wouldn't have pulled away from him.

"Stop overthinking," Clara spoke up. She gave him a gentle look. "She is fine. She got a good punch in, actually. And thanks to Alex, she got help. He flagged down a car and it happened to be an off-duty police officer."

He nodded, thankful for that.

"Can I see her?" he asked, his voice sounding choked.

"Only for a minute because she needs her rest," Nan spoke, giving him a thoughtful look. "Stop beating yourself up, Beau. You couldn't have known this was going to happen. Go in, check on her and you can figure all of this out another day."

Another day. He wanted another day with her. Maybe a year or possibly fifty. The moment he realized she'd been hurt and how badly it could have gone had someone not been there to help, it had made him aware that he needed this woman in his life. Forever.

"Room 110," Grayson told Beau as he got up.

A nurse came out as he opened the door to step inside.

"Keep the visit short," she warned. "Wash your hands and wear a mask."

"Got it." He stepped inside, stopping at the sink near the door to wash his hands and grab a mask from the dispenser.

He was surprised to find her watching him, her gray eyes pained, her jaw swollen and bruised. He bit back the many things he wanted to say, most of them about the future, a future that he longed to have with her.

"Stop looking at me that way," she whispered into the darkened room.

"What way?" he asked as he took a seat in the chair next to the bed.

"Like you think I'm broken. I'm not broken. I'm whole. Fairly whole, anyway."

"I know." He tamped down the words about his fears of losing her, about needing her in his life. All of the things he wanted to say.

"If I had gotten to my car a little quicker, got in and locked the door…"

"He was on meth. You can't predict what someone in his condition would do."

"I know." She closed her eyes and a tear trickled. "Poor Alex."

"What will happen to him?"

"He's been placed in a home," she said. "Pastor Matthews and his wife. They've never considered fostering, but Alex needs them."

"I need you in my life." The words slipped out and he wouldn't regret the admission.

She gave him a startled look. "What?"

"I need you in my life."

"No, you don't. I've been here for you while you were going through a pretty difficult situation. It's normal to think that this feels like something more than it is. Once you get back to your real life, you'll understand that better."

"Are you telling me how I feel?" he asked.

"No, I'm telling you like it is. This is an attachment formed because I was here for you after your friends' deaths. It isn't real."

"It is real." He felt as if he might lose control if she didn't stop denying what was between them. "What I feel for you is real."

She shook her head. "Someday you'll thank me for telling you to go away."

"I don't think so. I want you in my life. I want to…" He wanted to marry her, have children together, raise the girls together. But instead, he was losing her.

"When my father threw me in that basement, he broke my body in so many ways. It will take a medical miracle for me to have children. I might someday need a wheelchair. I don't think I'll make anyone a good wife, but I do know that I can help children to have better lives. I'm going to take the job at the residential facility."

This was the way their story had to end. He didn't want to accept it, but he could see that she wasn't going to relent.

He nodded, giving in and wishing he could argue her into seeing reason. She had her mind made up. She wanted to work in a facility hours from Pleasant. Meanwhile, his life was also taking a different path. He'd hoped their paths would intersect someday, not go in completely different directions.

Her hand reached for his, surprising him.

Seeing her in that bed, the bruises on her face, the paleness of her skin, he wanted to pick her up and hold her. He wanted to take her pain.

He'd never been in a situation where he felt more helpless, more lost. He prayed. He couldn't let go of the thought that God had brought them together to be a family.

Then she spoke softly in the pale light of the room.

"As time goes on, you'll see that I'm right, that we were friends for this season in your life when you needed someone, and it just happened to be. For me, it's been a time of forgiving, of letting go."

"I'm going to let you believe that, for now. But I'm going to keep praying and I'd ask you to do the same. Emery Guthrie, God is doing something here, between us. Don't miss it."

He kissed her cheek before he left the room and he didn't miss the tear that slid down her cheek. She thought she was saving him from something.

He didn't want her to save him from loving her.

Chapter Sixteen

Emery gathered up the gift for Charlie's birthday and the smaller gift for Cadence. Her heart sped up at the idea of seeing Beau and the girls. No, she wouldn't go riding. She would stop by, eat a piece of cake and give Charlie her gift. She was leaving Zeb at home so he wouldn't create a commotion with the horses. He'd sprawled out on the rug at Nan's feet and she occasionally dropped a piece of cookie for him.

Emery moved aside some papers as she worked on Charlie's gift, putting the ornate show bridle in a gift box and then taping it up.

Something on the paper caught her attention. She read over the legal jargon and then looked at Nan.

"What is this?"

Nan glanced up, all innocent. "I'm doing what I think is best for you all, for me, for him."

"Nan," Emery started, then she hesitated, not sure what to say. "It isn't my business."

"Isn't it?" Nan asked, sitting up a little straighter. "Emery, I love you with all my heart, but you're about the most stubborn girl I've ever met. That man loves you. He wants to spend time with you. He probably wants to marry you. I know the past the two of you share, but you can't let that come between you."

"It isn't about the past," Emery said, feeling crushed. "Nan, it's about the future. It's about life and babies and not wanting a man to ever feel like he has to take care of me."

"Like I said, stubborn girl. People who love each other take care of each other. The way I've taken care of you all and you girls are taking care of me. Where would I be if it wasn't for the people who love me?"

Nan's words tore at her heart. She blinked away the tears in her eyes and took a deep breath, trying to ground herself, to keep from falling apart.

"He loves you," Nan said. "And I know I miss plenty these days, but I believe you love him, too."

"I helped him because it was the right thing to do. I helped him because it felt like a healing path. I didn't mean to fall in love."

"But you did. Oh, the silly, fickle heart. A

person never knows what direction it might take." Nan slipped Zeb another piece of cookie and grinned, looking younger, more like herself. "I love you, Emery. I know you think you want a job hours from home. I know you think you can't have what you really want. But try. Try to take hold of whatever this is between you and Beau Wilde. Try giving God a chance to show you what might be rather than missing out on something wonderful all because you're afraid."

"Oh, Nan, I love you. And you're always right. I'm not sure if the job is what I really want or if it's a way to run from what I want."

"I think you know what you really want." Nan patted her cheek. "You want the boy."

"I'm afraid," Emery admitted.

"That's why I'm helping you. I'm signing this house and twenty acres over to you, on the condition that you continue to lease the workshop to Beau."

"That's very sneaky of you." Emery swiped at a tear that trickled down her cheek.

"Possibly," Nan said without any sign of remorse. "Let me point something out to you. Right now you're considering saying no to the job and you're feeling more at peace than you have in weeks."

Emery let the realization sink in. Nan had the right of it. She did, indeed, feel more at peace.

"Okay," she said, without actually admitting it.

"Because you're taking a moment and thinking about what could be and what God might want, rather than trying to make plans on your own, plans born out of a desperate need to escape."

Emery hugged her mother. "You're always right."

"I know," Nan said. "It's a gift. Go to Charlie's birthday party. When you get there, you're going to feel even more at peace. You're going to step into that man's life and realize it is like coming home. You see, years ago, I thought I wanted to be alone in this old house and I was miserable. One day I made a decision to take in some young girls who needed a home. God's peace washed over me. I'd found His path, His plan, and when you find that place, you find contentment."

"I love you," Emery said as she reached for the bag she'd place the gifts in, her purse and keys. She gathered it all up, slipped her arm into her crutch and turned to go.

"I love you," Nan said. "Tell Charlie I wish I could be there, but I'm afraid I couldn't last as long as you kids."

"I'll tell her."

"Emery," Nan called as Emery started out the door.

"Yes." Emery waited, afraid because Nan's voice no longer seemed sure.

"I want you to know, I might forget, but you won't." Nan drew in a breath. "The day I adopted you was one of the most blessed days of my life."

"It was the very best day of my life." Emery blinked away the moisture that gathered in her eyes. "We will both remember that."

"Go before we cry," Nan said. "Go tell that man that you love him."

Beau watched as Charlie sat with her small group of friends. They were taking turns on the tire swing he'd recently hung from an old oak tree in the backyard. Every now and then he'd hear a burst of laughter from them.

Charlie laughed and smiled, but on occasion her eyes would dart to the driveway. She was looking for Emery. He knew because he'd been doing the same, glancing that way when he heard a car on the road.

"You're ruining the birthday party," Grayson said as he came over to stand next to him at the grill.

"How do you figure?" Beau asked as he flipped the burgers. "Do these look like they're about ready for cheese?"

"Looks that way to me," Grayson said, not

really looking at the burgers. It was hot and the two of them were sweating up a storm. "Stop glaring at everyone."

"What?" Beau cut a corner of a burger to make sure it was cooked all the way through. "I'm not glaring, I'm cooking."

"And glaring. She isn't here. She probably isn't going to be here."

"She told Charlie she would come, so she will."

"Did she?" Grayson asked as he unwrapped cheese.

"She said she'd come to the party but she wouldn't go on the trail ride."

He finished the burgers and moved them to a tray. "We should feed this group before they get hangry," he said.

"Everyone looks pretty content. I'm the one who gets that way," Grayson admitted.

Beau carried the platter of burgers to the screened-in porch, safe from flies and mosquitoes. Cadence sat inside, curled up against Avery, who was reading her a book, using character voices to make the little girl giggle.

"Need help?" Avery asked, starting to move.

He set the tray on the table and put a hand up to stop her. "I've got this. You stay and read to Cadence. I'm not good at the voices."

"You'll learn."

"I hope."

Ethan came out of the house with a big tray that held side dishes, condiments and buns. "I think we've got everything."

"Thank you. I'll call everyone in." Beau opened the door, but the girls were already heading his way. Charlie led the group. She stopped to steal a glance in the direction of the road.

He didn't know what he should say about Emery's absence, or if he should say anything. He couldn't imagine her not showing up, not when she knew how important today was for Charlie and how much the girls needed her. He couldn't believe she would miss this day.

This first birthday without her parents would be a tough one. And in six months they would have the first Christmas. There would be many firsts for a very long time to come. He had to be prepared, better prepared than he'd been for this birthday, which he'd almost forgotten.

"She'll be here," he guaranteed.

"I don't think so," Charlie said with a shrug. "It's fine. After all, we're going to move and she won't be around."

"Yes, things will be different. But one thing, Charlie…"

Charlie's eyes lit up. "We won't be moving, will we? We're going to stay in Pleasant?"

He nodded and she grabbed him in a tight hug. "Thank you," she whispered.

"You're welcome. But there's more," he said. Then he saw her car. The rest would have to wait.

"Emery is here. Emery!" Out the door Charlie went.

Cadence went after her, scrambling to get shoes on her feet as she hurried out the door.

Beau followed, just as excited but knowing it would be a strange sight to see a grown man tearing across the yard. He leaned back in the door, remembering their guests. "Hey, you all help yourself to a burger."

Avery stood, putting Cadence's book on the table. "If that's my sister you all are chasing down, you be good to her, Beau Wilde."

"I promise."

"I'll get everyone fed," she offered, then called all of the girls to the serving table.

Beau walked pretty quickly across the yard in the direction of Emery's car. The girls were already there waiting for him. As he drew closer, he heard the sweetest sound ever.

"Emery, Emery, I can ride my pony." Cadence jumped up and down, waiting for Emery to close her car door. Charlie stood close by, talking so fast the words ran together.

Emery laughed and gathered the girls close,

dropping her bags and purse in the process. "I love you, girls."

Something had changed. He could feel the difference.

Emery spotted him, her gaze landing on his, a sweet smile spreading across her face. "Hey."

"Hey. How are you feeling?"

"Better," she said. "Much better."

"That's good."

They stood there waiting as the girls chattered on.

"We should join the party," Beau suggested to the girls. "Maybe give Emery a little space."

Charlie rolled her eyes. "But we missed her."

"You girls go on and we'll be there in a minute," Emery said as she pointed to the gift bag. "Charlie, can you grab that for me and take it to the house?"

"Is it for me?" Charlie started to peek.

"Don't peek," Emery warned. "Yes, the big gift is yours. The other is for Cadence. We'll be there in a minute."

Charlie looked from one to the other of them. "Is everything okay?"

Emery gave the girl a quick hug. "It's definitely okay."

Charlie motioned for her sister to follow. "Come on, Caddie, grown-up talk time."

The two girls left, but they kept glancing back as they walked.

"Everything is definitely okay?" he said as they stood there watching the girls leave.

"Mmm-hmm," she said. "You bought Nan's business. Why?"

"Well, I needed a change. I've never wanted to be in the car business. It was my dad's dream and now he wants to retire. We sold the dealerships to a bigger conglomerate. I decided to go into the johnboat business. Nan is going to teach me her craft."

"I see," she said as she leaned against her car.

He thought she probably didn't realize how beautiful she was. He thought he could spend a lifetime telling her all of the ways he found her beautiful. He would start with her compassion for others and work his way outward, to her dark hair with hints of auburn, to her gray eyes that were kind and expressive. The smile she didn't share often enough.

"I'm not taking the job," she said after a few minutes. "I realized I was running. From you. The idea of you scares me."

"The idea of me?" He was confused.

"The idea of loving and losing you. Or loving you and you not loving me back." She shrugged a little. "Foolish but true. I wanted to leave you before you could leave me."

He stepped in front of her so they were face-to-face. She raised her chin a notch and met his gaze. "I'd rather kiss you right now than do anything else."

"I'd like that," she said.

He wrapped an arm around her waist and drew her close. Her left hand touched his neck, encouraging him to linger on the kiss. Her lips were soft and she tasted like home.

"Emery, I love you," he whispered after they pulled away. They remained close and her hand had clasped his, holding tight.

"I love you, Beau. I'm afraid of what that love looks like or where it takes us, but I want to take the journey. With you. I want to see what God has planned for us."

"I'm raising two girls."

"I love those girls," she said, leaning her head against his shoulder. "I'm not sure where we go from here, but I know that I can't walk away from you."

He pulled her close. "I'm so glad, because I would have done everything in my power to convince you to give us a chance."

"Emery, come on!" The voice came from a few feet away.

They turned to see Cadence standing a short distance away, a grin on her face. Her strawberry blond curls were a halo around her pixie face and happiness reflected in her blue eyes.

They would be a family. Beau knew it in his heart, knew it the way he knew the sky was blue and God answered prayers.

"I'm coming," Emery told the little girl, holding out her free hand. "Let's go open gifts."

Cadence took her hand and the three of them walked back to the house.

Epilogue

Six months later, Emery stood in her bedroom at Nan's, still in awe at her life. Today she would marry Beau Wilde. They were having their wedding at Nan's, because Emery wanted their lives to start on this farm that they would call home, where they would raise Cadence, Charlie and any other children God brought into their lives.

After going to a specialist for a second opinion, Emery learned she would never have her own children. She was still coming to terms with the knowledge and accepting that God would give her a full life, a full heart and a full home. Maybe not a family in the traditional way, but it would be the family He planned and that would make it perfect.

"I'm not sure why you're rushing into this," Nan said as she straightened the veil on Emery's head. Nan's hands shook more than they used to. But in her eyes, Emery saw the mother who had always loved her, cared for her, nurtured her. There was love in those eyes, even on days when Nan didn't seem to really remember who she was speaking to. Even on days when she tried to read the paper and for some reason the words didn't quite make sense.

"Because we love each other and we want to start our lives together as soon as possible."

And because she wanted Nan fully present for their wedding. She wanted this day to go in Nan's memory book while Nan could still remember.

"I'm so glad you're mine," Nan said as she hugged her close. "You're all my girls, but you, Emery, you're the one that stuck. You're the one that I knew I had to give my last name. You needed that name."

Emery swiped away a tear. "Don't make me cry on my wedding day."

"You're getting married?" Nan closed her eyes for a moment, as if trying to ground herself to the moment, to the memory. "Yes, you are. I wonder if the girls will be here. I kept thinking my mother would come, but I don't think we got the invitation to her, did we?"

"We did mail all of the invitations," Emery said. She left it at that, because it wasn't necessary to remind Nan that her mother had been gone for years. There were times that Nan lived in the past, where those people were still alive and with her.

"I see. Oh, you're wearing my pearls."

"Yes, you told me they count for both something borrowed and something old." Emery turned to look at herself in the mirror. The door opened and Clara and Avery hurried in.

"We're getting everyone seated," Avery said. "Look how beautiful it is. A late fall wedding outside. It's a little cool, but the boat shop is cleaned up and ready for the reception. Mums and sunflowers make everything so autumnal."

Emery sneaked a peek out the window at the rows of chairs, the hay bales with the flowers stacked in decorative displays and the arch under which they would get married. Nan had used her woodworking skills to build a beautiful arch and they'd spent two days twining flowers and autumn leaves around the wood.

Charlie, Clara and Avery were her bridesmaids, and their dresses were shades of autumn red. Cadence was wearing a pretty golden dress and serving as the flower girl. Zeb had the honor of being the ring bearer. He seemed very proud of his red collar with the tiny bag tied with gold ribbon that would carry the rings.

"How's my groom?" she asked. She hadn't

seen him since the previous evening at the rehearsal.

"He's grinning from ear to ear," Clara told her. "I'm not sure if he can wait five more minutes to take your hand in his."

"I love him so much," Emery said as she peeked out the window one last time.

"He loves you," Nan said. "Oh, honey, I'm so proud. I'm so glad I'm here. Thank you for this wedding."

"Thank you," Emery said as her sisters came to stand behind her. "The three of us want you to know how much we love you, Nan, and how grateful we are that God gave us you."

Avery whistled and the door opened. The photographer entered.

"Time for photos," she said. She captured the four of them and then Charlie and Cadence joined them for a quick picture. Nan pulled the veil down and another picture was taken.

"It's time," Avery said. "Ready, girls?"

Emery nodded. She was ready.

The bridal party exited Nan's house and Emery waited with Nan, watching as her bridesmaids walked down the aisle accompanied by Beau's groomsmen. Cadence led Zeb, the two being very solemn until the end when someone tossed a dog biscuit. Zeb snapped it up and kept walking.

Emery walked down the aisle on that perfectly sunny but cool autumn day to a song about being joined to the one meant for her, the one who might have been missed had there not been God. Nan walked next to her in a pretty red floral dress, holding tight to Emery's arm, tears trickling down her cheeks as she gave away another daughter, and Emery knew Nan prayed that she would remember.

Her eyes connected with Beau's. She couldn't help but smile. He stood there so tall and handsome, so sure and strong. He was a man of faith, a man of conviction. He was hers. God had created them for this moment, this love and this life together.

Beau held her hands in his, her crutch not needed as long as he held her, sharing his strength.

"I love you," he said. "I love you and I'm so blessed that God gave you to me, as wife, as mother to the girls. I'll cherish you and care for you because that is what God has called me to do. I'll love you always and forever, because that is what my heart is called to do."

They said their "I dos," and then Pastor Matthews pronounced them husband and wife. And they kissed, there under the arch that Nan had made with loving hands.

Emery held tight to Beau, knowing she would hold tight to him for the rest of her life. Today they started their journey together, in front of God and the people gathered to celebrate with them.

Today wasn't the end. It was the beginning.

* * * * *

*If you loved this story,
pick up these other books
from much-loved author Brenda Minton*

Reunited with the Rancher
The Rancher's Christmas Match
Her Oklahoma Rancher
"His Christmas Family"
in Western Christmas Wishes
The Rancher's Holiday Hope
The Prodigal Cowboy
The Rancher's Holiday Arrangement
Her Small Town Secret
Her Christmas Dilemma

*Available now from Love Inspired!
Find more great reads at
www.LoveInspired.com*

Dear Reader,

Thank you for hanging out with me in Pleasant, Missouri. I grew up on the James River, wading the cool waters, canoeing in the summer and camping along the riverbank.

I'm so thankful that my life has included those simple times, and I hope that as you read these books set in Pleasant, you find some of that peace, that time of reflection that I've found on the banks of the James.

In *Earning Her Trust*, we journey some rather troubled waters with the hero and heroine. Emery Guthrie's childhood left her physically and emotionally broken. Beau Wilde lived a charmed life, not thinking about how his actions and words hurt others. The two come together in a journey of healing and forgiveness that will change both of their lives forever. In a story that is as winding as our Missouri river, the two will find peace and a new path.

I hope you enjoy this last story in the Pleasant series!

I love hearing from readers. Contact me at minton.author@gmail.com, find me on Facebook at Brenda Minton, and check out my website at brendaminton.net.

Brenda

Get 4 FREE REWARDS!

We'll send you 2 FREE Books plus 2 FREE Mystery Gifts.

FREE
Value Over
$20

Both the **Love Inspired®** and **Love Inspired® Suspense** series feature compelling novels filled with inspirational romance, faith, forgiveness, and hope.

YES! Please send me 2 FREE novels from the Love Inspired or Love Inspired Suspense series and my 2 FREE gifts (gifts are worth about $10 retail). After receiving them, if I don't wish to receive any more books, I can return the shipping statement marked "cancel." If I don't cancel, I will receive 6 brand-new Love Inspired Larger-Print books or Love Inspired Suspense Larger-Print books every month and be billed just $5.99 each in the U.S. or $6.24 each in Canada. That is a savings of at least 17% off the cover price. It's quite a bargain! Shipping and handling is just 50¢ per book in the U.S. and $1.25 per book in Canada.* I understand that accepting the 2 free books and gifts places me under no obligation to buy anything. I can always return a shipment and cancel at any time. The free books and gifts are mine to keep no matter what I decide.

Choose one: ☐ **Love Inspired**
Larger-Print
(122/322 IDN GNWC)

☐ **Love Inspired Suspense**
Larger-Print
(107/307 IDN GNWN)

Name (please print)

Address   Apt. #

City   State/Province   Zip/Postal Code

Email: Please check this box ☐ if you would like to receive newsletters and promotional emails from Harlequin Enterprises ULC and its affiliates. You can unsubscribe anytime.

Mail to the Harlequin Reader Service:
IN U.S.A.: P.O. Box 1341, Buffalo, NY 14240-8531
IN CANADA: P.O. Box 603, Fort Erie, Ontario L2A 5X3

Want to try 2 free books from another series! Call 1-800-873-8635 or visit www.ReaderService.com.

---

*Terms and prices subject to change without notice. Prices do not include sales taxes, which will be charged (if applicable) based on your state or country of residence. Canadian residents will be charged applicable taxes. Offer not valid in Quebec. This offer is limited to one order per household. Books received may not be as shown. Not valid for current subscribers to the Love Inspired or Love Inspired Suspense series. All orders subject to approval. Credit or debit balances in a customer's account(s) may be offset by any other outstanding balance owed by or to the customer. Please allow 4 to 6 weeks for delivery. Offer available while quantities last.

Your Privacy—Your information is being collected by Harlequin Enterprises ULC, operating as Harlequin Reader Service. For a complete summary of the information we collect, how we use this information and to whom it is disclosed, please visit our privacy notice located at corporate.harlequin.com/privacy-notice. From time to time we may also exchange your personal information with reputable third parties. If you wish to opt out of this sharing of your personal information, please visit readerservice.com/consumerschoice or call 1-800-873-8635. **Notice to California Residents**—Under California law, you have specific rights to control and access your data. For more information on these rights and how to exercise them, visit corporate.harlequin.com/california-privacy.

LIRLIS22

Get 4 FREE REWARDS!

We'll send you 2 FREE Books plus 2 FREE Mystery Gifts.

FREE
Value Over
$20

Both the **Harlequin® Special Edition** and **Harlequin® Heartwarming™** series feature compelling novels filled with stories of love and strength where the bonds of friendship, family and community unite.

YES! Please send me 2 FREE novels from the Harlequin Special Edition or Harlequin Heartwarming series and my 2 FREE gifts (gifts are worth about $10 retail). After receiving them, if I don't wish to receive any more books, I can return the shipping statement marked "cancel." If I don't cancel, I will receive 6 brand-new Harlequin Special Edition books every month and be billed just $4.99 each in the U.S or $5.74 each in Canada, a savings of at least 17% off the cover price or 4 brand-new Harlequin Heartwarming Larger-Print books every month and be billed just $5.74 each in the U.S. or $6.24 each in Canada, a savings of at least 21% off the cover price. It's quite a bargain! Shipping and handling is just 50¢ per book in the U.S. and $1.25 per book in Canada.* I understand that accepting the 2 free books and gifts places me under no obligation to buy anything. I can always return a shipment and cancel at any time. The free books and gifts are mine to keep no matter what I decide.

Choose one: ☐ **Harlequin Special Edition**
(235/335 HDN GNMP)
☐ **Harlequin Heartwarming Larger-Print**
(161/361 HDN GNPZ)

Name (please print)

Address   Apt. #

City   State/Province   Zip/Postal Code

Email: Please check this box ☐ if you would like to receive newsletters and promotional emails from Harlequin Enterprises ULC and its affiliates. You can unsubscribe anytime.

Mail to the **Harlequin Reader Service:**
IN U.S.A.: P.O. Box 1341, Buffalo, NY 14240-8531
IN CANADA: P.O. Box 603, Fort Erie, Ontario L2A 5X3

Want to try 2 free books from another series! Call 1-800-873-8635 or visit www.ReaderService.com.

COUNTRY LEGACY COLLECTION

Cowboys, adventure and romance await you in this new collection! Enjoy superb reading all year long with books by bestselling authors like Diana Palmer, Sasha Summers and Marie Ferrarella!

YES! Please send me the **Country Legacy Collection!** This collection begins with 3 FREE books and 2 FREE gifts in the first shipment. Along with my 3 free books, I'll also get 3 more books from the **Country Legacy Collection**, which I may either return and owe nothing or keep for the low price of $24.60 U.S./$28.12 CDN each plus $2.99 U.S./$7.49 CDN for shipping and handling per shipment*. If I decide to continue, about once a month for 8 months, I will get 6 or 7 more books but will only pay for 4. That means 2 or 3 books in every shipment will be FREE! If I decide to keep the entire collection, I'll have paid for only 32 books because 19 are FREE! I understand that accepting the 3 free books and gifts places me under no obligation to buy anything. I can always return a shipment and cancel at any time. My free books and gifts are mine to keep no matter what I decide.

☐ 275 HCK 1939   ☐ 475 HCK 1939

_____
Name (please print)

_____
Address   Apt. #

_____
City   State/Province   Zip/Postal Code

> Mail to the **Harlequin Reader Service:**
> **IN U.S.A.:** P.O. Box 1341, Buffalo, NY 14240-8571
> **IN CANADA:** P.O. Box 603, Fort Erie, Ontario L2A 5X3